A MIGHTY **MARVEL** CHAPTER BOOK

ASTONISHING ADVENTURES!

3 Books in 1

Spider-Man: Attack of the Heroes and *Captain America: The Tomorrow Army* originally published in 2014 by Marvel Press, an imprint of Disney Book Group.

Iron Man: Invasion of the Space Phantoms originally published in 2016 by Marvel Press, an imprint of Disney Book Group.

SPIDER-MAN
ATTACK OF THE HEROES
PAGE 1

CAPTAIN AMERICA
THE TOMORROW ARMY
PAGE 127

IRON MAN
INVASION OF THE SPACE PHANTOMS
PAGE 269

MARVEL
Los Angeles
New York

ATTA

OF THE HEROES

STARRING
SPIDER-MAN

BY RICH THOMAS JR.

ILLUSTRATED BY
RON LIM AND LEE DUHIG

Los Angeles
New York

FEATURING YOUR FAVORITES!

Kid from Queens

The crush

PETER PARKER

SPIDER-MAN

Gwen's dad

CAPTAIN STACY

GWEN STACY

DAREDEVIL

NOVA

VIBRANIUM???

CAP'S SHIELD

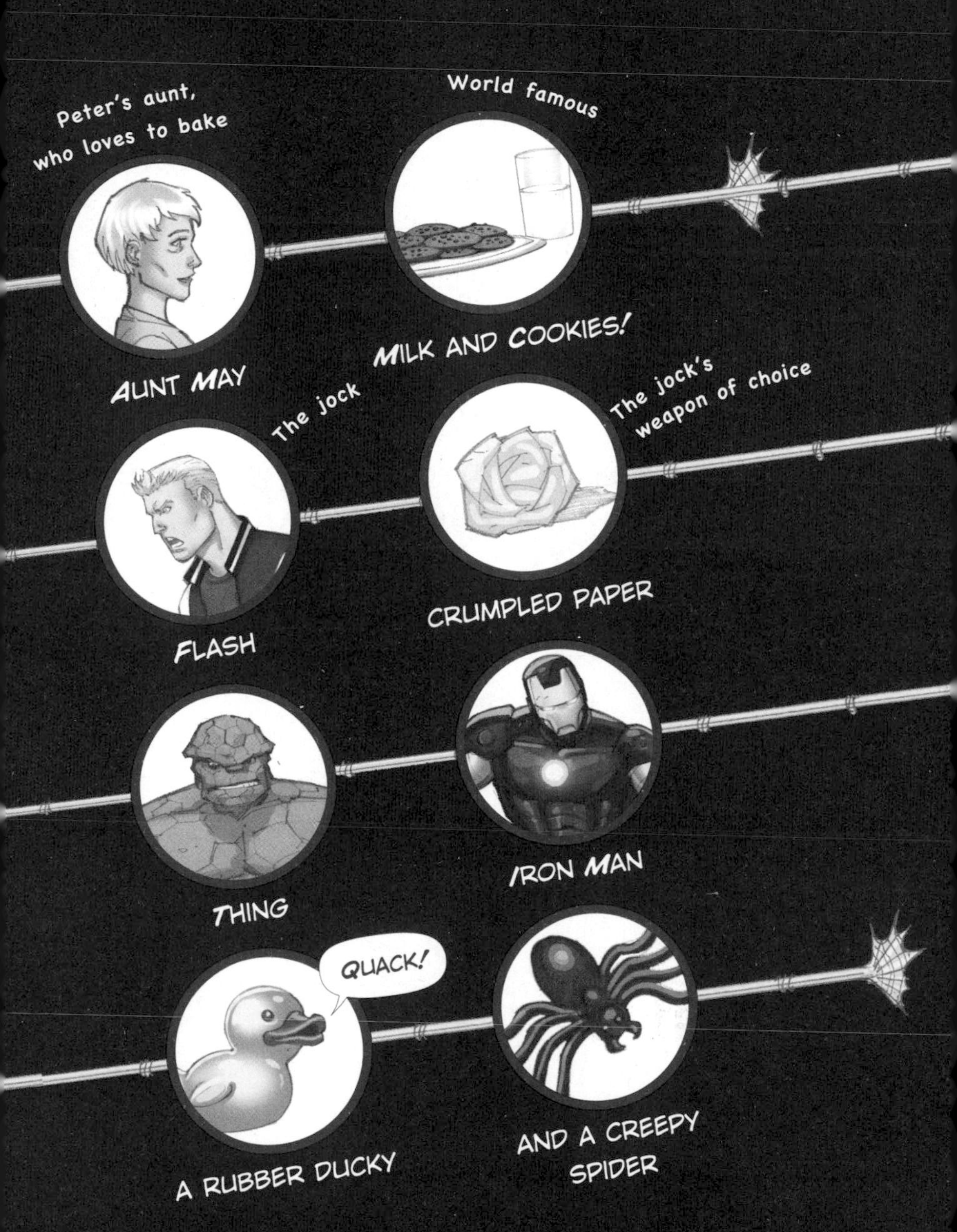
Peter's aunt, who loves to bake
AUNT MAY
World famous
MILK AND COOKIES!
The jock
FLASH
The jock's weapon of choice
CRUMPLED PAPER
THING
IRON MAN
QUACK!
A RUBBER DUCKY
AND A CREEPY SPIDER

THE STORY OF SPIDER-MAN

*P*eter Parker was just an average kid who loved science. While attending a presentation about radiation, he was bitten by a radioactive spider. This bite gave Peter amazing abilities. He could cling to walls, leap like a spider, and sense danger.

Peter used his scientific knowledge to create sticky fluid and web-shooters. With these
he could spin webs and swing from skyscraper
to skyscraper high above the streets of New
York City. He created a costume and called
himself

SPIDER-MAN!

One night, Peter's beloved uncle Ben was killed by a burglar—a burglar Spider-Man could have stopped earlier that night but had decided not to. Peter was devastated. But he remembered something Uncle Ben had always told him: **WITH GREAT POWER COMES GREAT RESPONSIBILITY.**

He would never again pass up an opportunity to help. From that day on, Peter used his powers to fight for justice and defend the public. He stopped everything from petty thieves to Super Villains.

Peter has had countless amazing adventures since becoming Spider-Man. This is just one of them. . . .

CHAPTER

"**D**on't look up, don't look up, don't look up," Peter Parker mumbled. He squinted and tried to will away what was coming toward him.

"Hey, bookworm!" Flash Thompson called out from the other end of the hall. Peter looked up from his locker. Flash was Midtown High's quarterback and was always followed by a group of other jocks and adoring cheerleaders.

"**THINK FAST!**" Flash said as he tossed a balled-up piece of loose-leaf paper at Peter. It

bounced off his forehead and into his locker.

"Real funny, Eugene," Peter said. He never called "Flash" by his nickname, because he knew the jock hated his *real* name. "Maybe if you used paper for something other than throwing, you'd actually graduate high school before you're a senior citizen," Peter quipped.

"And maybe if you spent less time studying

and more time *RELAXING*, you'd have better luck with the ladies," Flash said, motioning to the giggling cheerleaders several lockers away.

"Luck, huh? Glad that's something you think you have, because it's all you've got," Peter shot back.

Flash waved his hand in the air to dismiss Peter. But Peter could tell by the look in Flash's eye that his comment had stung.

"Come on, crew. Let's not waste any more time with this loser," Flash said. Then he and his fan club headed down the hall.

Peter picked up the crumpled paper from

the floor of his locker. He opened it. Even though he wasn't surprised at what he saw there, he had to admit that it still bothered him.

He tossed the paper into the recycling bin. Flash shot a look back at Peter over his shoulder. By his smile, Peter could tell that Flash had seen him open the paper and throw it away. And the worst part was that Flash seemed to be enjoying every second of it. If Peter thought he'd stuck it to Flash before with his comment about Flash's need for luck, it was Flash who had the last laugh—as usual.

Flash and Peter went their separate ways—Flash to the schoolyard and Peter to the school library. Maybe Flash was right. Maybe Peter *did* spend too much time studying and not enough having fun. After all, it was lunchtime, and the rest of his class was outside enjoying the beautiful late-fall weather. He was holed up in the stuffy school library, preparing for the next week's science test. And he was the only one in there.

Well, *almost* the only one.

"HEY, PETE!" Gwen Stacy said.

"SHHH!" the school librarian scolded.

"I thought I was the only one who spent my lunchtime studying," she whispered.

"Even a girl as smart as you has to be wrong sometimes," Peter said, and he thought he saw Gwen blush a little.

"Well, I couldn't ask for better company," she replied.

Then it was Peter's turn to squirm uncomfortably. He set his books down next to her and took a seat. If Flash could see him now! For once Peter was happy to be a bit of an outsider. In this case it meant he got to spend time alone with Gwen Stacy. There was no way any other kid in his class would be joining them. Who else would pass up the beautiful weather for a study session?

Then the library door creaked open, and Peter couldn't believe what he saw.

FLASH was on his way in. What could he be doing in a library? Smiling, he slowly walked over to where Peter and Gwen were sitting.

"Hey, bookworm, I noticed you **dropped** this," Flash said, and handed Peter the drawing he'd thrown out just a few minutes earlier. There it was in plain sight. And

HHHHHHHH!!!!

Gwen was staring at it, too. What would she think? Would she find it funny? Would she laugh at him?

Peter **ripped** the paper off the table and grabbed his books.

"I've got to go," he said, and pushed the chair back, maybe a little too hard.

"**SHHHHHHH!!!**"

the librarian said again.

"But I was just doing my good deed for the day!" Flash said sarcastically.

"You wouldn't know a good deed if it hit you like a ton of bricks!" Peter replied, imagining a ton of bricks falling onto Flash.

"How would you know about a ton of *anything*? You're such a weakling you couldn't even lift a *pound!*" Flash said.

Peter stormed out of the room and slammed the door behind him.

"SHHHHHHH!!!!"

the librarian said so loudly that Peter could hear him through the closed door.

Peter was shaking.

He was *hurt*.

He was *embarrassed*.

But most of all he was **angry**!

CHAPTER

*P*eter spent the rest of the day distracted. In chemistry lab, his teacher noticed that he was not quite himself.

"Can anyone tell me the symbol for gold on the periodic table of elements?" the teacher asked.

When no one could answer, he turned to Peter, hoping his star student would know.

"Peter?" he asked.

"Huh? Oh . . ." Peter said. "Sorry, what were you asking?"

His teacher looked deflated.

"The symbol for gold. On the periodic table," the teacher repeated.

"UMMM, G???" Peter answered.

"*AU. AU* is the symbol for gold," the teacher said with disappointment.

And Peter was disappointed, too. He didn't like anyone getting the better of him. And Flash was certainly doing just that. He had him so down that Peter couldn't even concentrate in his favorite class. He couldn't even remember the most obvious answers.

But he did remember that piece of paper with the drawing and how he'd felt when Gwen saw it. Peter just wanted that day to end!

The bell **rang,** signaling the end of the school day. Peter made his way to his locker to collect his things.

"Pete!" someone called from behind him.

He turned to see Gwen.

"Hey, I just wanted to say that I think what Flash did before was a bit mean," she said.

"Yeah, well, I don't let it get to me," Peter replied, trying to smile.

"It sure doesn't look that way," Gwen said. "You're not your upbeat self. Don't let that jerk get to you. You'll be the one laughing when you've won a Nobel Prize and he's still repeating sophomore year."

Peter tried to imagine this.

"Thanks," he said, forcing a smile.

"You're welcome," she said, grinning. "Want

to go hang out at the Queensboro Coffee Shoppe? We can finish up our studying. Pick up where we left off in the library?"

Peter thought about it. It sure was tempting. But he knew he might not be the best company right now. He was in a really bad mood, after all. And besides, what if Flash busted in on them again? Peter was sure he wouldn't be able to hold back. And he couldn't hit Flash. Peter packed an unusually powerful **PUNCH.**

SWoooOooSH!

"I wish I could," Peter said. "But I promised Aunt May that I'd run a few errands before I got home."

Gwen looked disappointed, but understood. Peter searched for things to grab from his locker and paused, his eyes landing on his gym bag. Then, as Gwen walked away, he snatched it and made his way up to the school's top floor.

Peter looked around to make sure the coast was clear. Then he slipped into a small supply closet that he knew hadn't been used in years.

He unzipped his bag and took out his famous red and blue mask, gloves, and boots. He always wore the rest of his costume under his street clothes, just in case he needed a quick change. He put on the rest of his costume and relied on his special power—his spider-sense—to warn him if anyone was around.

Confident, Peter sneaked up the stairs to the rooftop and pointed his wrists at the school's clock tower. Then he shot streams of webs from his web-shooters, and faster than anyone could notice, he swung out over Queens toward the city.

Being Spider-Man didn't mean Peter didn't have to deal with the same problems as ordinary teenagers. But it did give him unique ways of blowing off steam. One of his favorite ways was using his webbing to swing over the rooftops of New York and through the sky-scraper canyons of Fifth Avenue.

Spider-Man swung his way to the Queens cable car that ran over the Queensboro Bridge into Manhattan. He shot his webbing at a car and hitched a ride under the cab into the city. The wall-crawler would make it to Manhattan in no time!

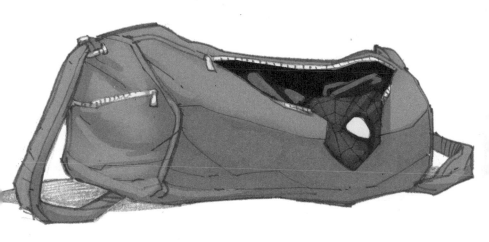

"Woo-hoo!!!!"

Peter hooted as he swung over the East River.
There were few things that made him happier
than this. He climbed up the side of the car
and noticed a little boy looking out over the
skyline with his hands against the window.
Peter waved at the surprised kid, who smiled
and waved back. The boy tugged on his dad's

shirt, but before the man turned around, Peter was gone. He'd leaped off the cab and was swinging between skyscrapers and springing from water towers.

Soon he was in Central Park, swinging from the trees and enjoying the crisp fall air. He noticed people running and biking on the park trails, pointing up at him in amazement as he swung by. A little boy dropped his ice cream as he watched his favorite Super Hero swing right overhead. Everything was so different when he was dressed as Spider-Man. People were interested in him. They were excited when they saw him. They grabbed their smartphones and snapped pictures. It wasn't like school at all.

Peter looked down and saluted his fans. He loved the attention.

But being Spider-Man wasn't all about having fun. And Peter was reminded of this when his spider-sense began to *tingle*.

"Of course," Peter said. "Nothing like a problem to spoil a perfect afternoon."

As he continued to swing through Central Park, he looked for any sign of trouble. Then he noticed lights flashing from police cars.

There were at least a dozen of them parked at odd angles in front of the

Museum of Natural History. Then he looked up and couldn't believe his eyes.

"What's going on?" he said.

Daredevil, another Super Hero, whom Spider-Man had worked with a bunch of times, was swinging away from the scene. Daredevil had a special extending billy club that he used to swing around the city the same way Spider-Man used his webs.

Daredevil turned around.

"SPIDER-MAN!" he said, looking at Peter.

Peter noticed Daredevil's glance. He must have been using his other senses to spot Spider-Man. After all, as Spidey knew, Daredevil was blind. No matter what had tipped him off, Daredevil started to flee over the city. Spider-Man chased after him. Both of the

heroes swung through alleyways, over roof-tops, across bridges, and through tunnels until Spidey finally caught up with Daredevil to confront him.

"Hey, **DD,** what's up?" Spider-Man asked. He looked down. "Other than us, obviously."

Daredevil gritted his teeth and took a swing at Spider-Man with his billy club.

"Whoa. You in a bad mood or something?" Spider-Man asked.

Daredevil just grunted and swung at him again.

"Um, okay, if it's a fight you're looking for . . ." Spider-Man said, then lifted his wrists and shot webbing at Daredevil, and the pair began to struggle in midair!

In the clash, Spider-Man noticed something fall from Daredevil's belt. He shot a web to snatch whatever it

was. And in that moment of distraction he allowed Daredevil to escape.

Peter looked at the object he'd caught. It just looked like a chunk of metal—very heavy metal, but still metal. And if it came from the Museum of Natural History, it must be valuable. Peter rushed back to the gathered officers. He might have lost Daredevil, but he got something in return.

CHAPTER 3

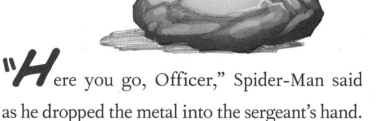

Vibranium

"**H**ere you go, Officer," Spider-Man said as he dropped the metal into the sergeant's hand.

"Wow, you Super Hero types never stop surprising me. One of you steals something, another one brings it back," the cop said.

"Honestly, I'm not sure what's going on. The guy who got away is usually on our side," Spider-Man replied.

"We know. Daredevil's helped us before, too," the sergeant said. "But he's now wanted for questioning."

None of this was making sense.

"Well, got to run—or **SWING,** I should say," Spider-Man said. "Hey, before I go, what's so special about that chunk of metal?"

"It's from the Vibranium exhibit at the museum," the sergeant said. "It's the strongest metal on earth. Really rare. Captain America's shield is made from it. Better hope Cap doesn't go bad. This stuff would hurt if it was thrown at you!"

"Yikes!" Spider-Man said, not wanting to think about it. He waved to the officers, who thanked him; then he swung off across the river toward home. By the time he got there, the sun was setting. He swooped down behind his garage and changed out of his costume.

"Peter! I was worried about you!" Aunt May said when he finally walked into the house. "Where have you been?"

Aunt May had always been edgy. But she'd been worse since Uncle Ben died. She often thought the worst when Peter was running late. Peter kissed her on the cheek and smiled, which always made her smile, too.

"I'm sorry, Aunt May," Peter said. "I lost track of time studying after school, and then I got stuck on the train. I didn't have service in the tunnel, so I couldn't call."

Peter didn't like lying to Aunt May, but he couldn't ever tell her the truth. He couldn't tell her he was the amazing **SPIDER-MAN**.

"I'm just glad you're home," she said, squeezing his hand.

After dinner, Peter went up to his room to do his homework and was soon ready for bed. But he had a lot of trouble sleeping. He

wondered why Daredevil had stolen the Vibranium. He worried about his upcoming science test.

Before he knew it, morning had arrived and it was time for school again. He wasn't sure how much he'd slept, or if he'd even slept at all. He felt like a robot going through the motions as he showered, brushed his teeth, and got ready for school.

"See you later, Aunt May," he said between yawns as he left the house.

"Peter!" his aunt called after him. "You forgot this," she said, standing at the door, holding his backpack. "You know, studying is great and important, but if you study too hard you'll just exhaust yourself."

Peter pecked her on the cheek and continued on to the subway, which he rode to school, completely wiped out from the night before.

"Hey, look who it is!" Flash shouted as Peter walked into Midtown High.

"Not in the mood," Peter replied.

"Bookworm's 'not in the mood,'" Flash teased.

Peter opened his locker and yawned.

"Tired, Parker? What, was the Math-lete World Series on last night? Went into extra innings?" Flash said, elbowing his buddies for a laugh.

"Hey, check this out," one of Flash's friends said. "Somebody's posted another angle." He held up his smartphone, and there was a clip of Spider-Man battling Daredevil. Peter's fight had gone viral!

"Ooᵒoooh!!!!!"

"DUDE, LET ME SEE THAT,"

Flash said, grabbing the phone from his friend. "Man, he's freaking amazing. Send me this link. I want to print out some of those pictures and put them up in my locker. Maybe that's what I'll major in when I get to college—Super Hero. You can do that, right?"

Anytime anyone talked about Spider-Man around Peter, he became uncomfortable. He couldn't let anyone find out he was Spider-Man. So he never knew how to react.

"I don't think any of them go to college," Peter said. He was immediately sorry he said it.

"Huh?" Flash said.

"I don't think Super Heroes go to college. I think they're a bunch of dopes. I don't trust any of them," Peter said, not sure how to get out of the conversation without bringing more attention to himself and to Spider-Man. He felt himself blush a little at being put on the spot. Of course he didn't believe these things, but if the other guys thought he hated Super Heroes, they'd never discover he *was* one.

"*HOHOHA!*"

Flash laughed. "I think Petey here is scared of Spider-Man! Is that it? Is Petey-weety afwaid of spiders?" he said in a babyish voice, making "Itsy-Bitsy Spider" gestures with his hands.

Peter slapped his hands away.

"OUCH!" Flash shouted genuinely, grabbing one of his hands where Peter had hit him. Peter had held back his strength, but even a light tap from Spider-Man was going to sting a little. Still, Flash tried to make it look like he wasn't hurt.

As he walked away he shouted down the hall, "Better be careful, Petey. Spider-Man is going to get you! Bwahahaha!"

As Flash moved on to his class, Peter couldn't help burying his face in his locker and cracking a smile.

CHAPTER 4

On his way to his next class, Peter bumped into Gwen.

"Pete!" she said, smiling at him.

"Oh, hi, Gwen," Peter responded, smiling back.

"Hey, I just got an alert on my phone that says they have Wall Street blocked off. Some sort of thing going on at the stock exchange," Gwen said, looking concerned.

"My dad works down there," she continued. "I hope he's okay. I texted him but haven't heard back yet." Gwen's father was a captain in the New York City Police Department.

Peter's first thought was that he'd throw on his Spider-Man costume and swing down to the stock exchange to see what was up. He had actually almost moved to jump away from Gwen and up to the roof. Whenever he heard about trouble, his first thought was always to run off and check it out, and then help if he could.

But he stopped himself this time. He was there at school to learn. He couldn't run off every time he heard something *might* be wrong.

"Did they say what was going on?" Peter asked.

"Nope," Gwen answered. "Just some news that blocks were roped off in the area."

Peter decided to wait until he had more information. After all, the city was protected by one of the world's top police forces. They could easily solve most of the city's problems. And if it seemed like they could use a hand, he'd be there as fast as possible.

"Well, let me know what's up," Peter said.

"I'm sure everything's fine. You'll hear back from your dad soon. He's just got to be busy with everything that's going on down there."

"I hope so," Gwen replied.

For the next two hours, Peter couldn't keep himself focused on his schoolwork. He stared out windows, looking for police helicopters or other Super Heroes rushing toward downtown Manhattan. He fought the urge to go check out the scene. It was in his nature.

Then, just before the dismissal bell rang, Peter heard two kids in his English class whispering about the scene downtown.

If there was any truth to that at all, Peter had to get involved.

Right after the bell rang Peter headed into Manhattan. He sneaked off the school grounds without anyone seeing him and swung quickly under the tracks of the elevated number 7 subway line on his way to downtown.

Before him was the New York Stock Exchange, and standing on top of it was his fellow Super Hero—and his good friend—Nova!

CHAPTER 5

Okay, now I know something's up, Spider-Man thought.

He didn't know Daredevil all that well. Sure, he knew enough to say that he was one of the good guys. But he couldn't say he was totally, 100 percent, absolutely sure he'd never go over to the other side and become a Super Villain. But Spider-Man had fought beside Nova a bunch of times, and the two heroes had become pretty good friends.

"HEY, NOVA!"

Spider-Man
shouted as he
swung by. "Not sure
what's going on here, but
I'm sure it's all a great
big misunderstanding. . . ."

"Spider-Man!" Nova said.
He even *sounded* like a villain.

"Yeah, it's me, Spider-
Man, your fellow Super *Hero*, buddy."

Nova lifted his hand and shot a blast at
Spider-Man.

"Um, are you mad at me or something? If it has to do with that five bucks I didn't lend you for a sports drink a few weeks ago, I swear, I really didn't have it on me. . . . Yikes!" Spider-Man jumped out of the way as Nova sent another blast in his direction.

Meanwhile, Spider-Man's *spider-sense* was tingling like crazy. He looked down and saw that the police were trained on him as well. It looked like the entire police force was gathered below. There were sirens blaring and lights flashing all over.

SPIDER-MAN AND NOVA, THIS IS CAPTAIN STACY OF THE NEW YORK CITY POLICE DEPARTMENT. SURRENDER YOURSELVES AND YOU WILL NOT BE HURT!

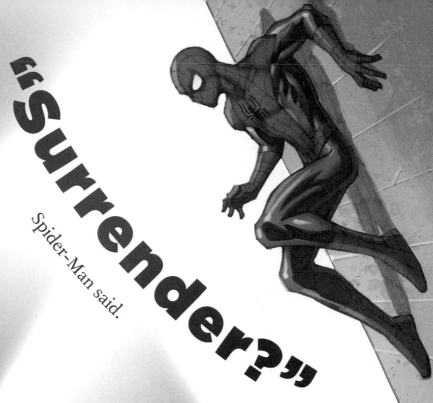

"Surrender?"

Spider-Man said.

"I figured you, or some other costumed creep, would try to stop me," said Nova. "So I already warned the cops. I told them to expect other Super Heroes to arrive."

"They think we're working together?" Spider-Man asked, shocked.

Nova smiled. "Yep, exactly as I set it up. Worked like a charm. So, what do you say, Spidey? They already think you're a criminal. Why not reap the benefits and work with me here?" Nova asked.

"Have you lost your mind? Oh, sorry, obvious question," Spider-Man replied. "You clearly *have*."

"Come on, Spidey, if you can't beat me, then join me," Nova replied.

"No way, no how, pal. I have no idea what's gotten into you, or Daredevil, but I'm going to figure it out," Spider-Man said.

"Spider-Man and Nova, we are giving you another **SIXTY SECONDS** to surrender. We're prepared to act if you won't come peacefully," Captain Stacy announced.

"They're going to get you one way or another," Nova said. "If you try to run, they'll think you're in this with me anyway. Or you can help me and actually get something out of it."

"What do you want here, anyway?" Spider-Man asked.

"THIRTY SECONDS!"

Captain Stacy shouted.

"Will you help me?" Nova said.

"It depends," Spider-Man replied. "What do I have to do?"

Nova smiled. "The building has been evacuated. Through the third-floor window on the northeast corner, you'll see a notebook computer. It will help us hack into any financial

system in the world. We can divert funds. Grab it and I'll split whatever I snag with you."

"So that's what you're up to!" Spider-Man said, proud of himself for tricking Nova into telling him. "Thanks for the tip!"

"FIFTEEN SECONDS!"

Spider-Man swooped around behind Nova and fired his webs at him, turning him into a Super Hero cocoon! Nova was fastened tightly to the roof, and Spider-Man was getting ready to move in for questioning when he heard Captain Stacy yell from below:

"TIME'S UP!!!"

Before Spider-Man could do anything else, rockets filled with some sort of gas started to streak around him. He began to cough but was able to dodge the pellets with his super skills. He weaved his way around their paths and swooped into the third-floor window Nova had mentioned. He webbed the notebook and grabbed it, shoving it under his arm, and swung back outside.

The cops were still firing their gas, so Spider-Man took a deep breath and swung down over their heads, avoiding it. He dropped the notebook to Captain Stacy.

"That's what he was looking for!"

Spider-Man shouted down to them as they continued to try to stop him. "Keep it safe!"

Captain Stacy looked up at Spider-Man skeptically. Peter nodded as if to say "Honest, Captain!" Captain Stacy looked down at the laptop.

Maybe Spider-Man is on our side, Captain Stacy thought.

Spider-Man saluted the cops, then shot a web at the flagpole on top of Federal Hall across the street and swung away. He took a quick look back at the stock exchange and saw Nova streak up into the sky and out of sight.

He must have slipped away while the cops were focused on me! Peter said to himself. Zero for two—first Daredevil gets away, now Nova. You're not doing too well here, Spidey.

Just when Peter thought he was clear, he heard police choppers overhead.

You have to hand it to those guys—they don't give up easily! he thought.

The copters swiveled and swerved to keep

track of him. But like an acrobat he tumbled and darted all over the city streets. When he was sure he was out of the copters' views, he slipped into an alleyway. He couldn't walk back out in his costume. But he didn't have anything to change into.

Spidey frantically took off his mask and made his way out of the alley, walking proudly in a suit of webbed-together garbage bags and a newspaper fedora.

He started walking down the street, hardly noticing the sideways glances he was getting. After all, to a guy who spends a lot of time swinging around the city in a red-and-blue suit, walking around in garbage bags was no sweat at all.

Two businessmen walked by and gave Peter a strange look. Peter tipped his hat to them and walked on. But he could still hear their conversation.

"MAN, PEOPLE ARE GET-TING WEIRDER AND WEIRDER IN THIS CITY. Did you hear what's going on down at the stock exchange?" one of the businessmen asked his friend.

"Yeah, and now they're saying Spider-Man's involved, too," the other replied. "I never trusted those guys anyway. You ask me, they're too dangerous to be out there."

Peter shook his head. Two heroes—Nova and Daredevil—had gone bad, Spider-Man looked like a villain, a bully was bothering him at school, and the girl he was crushing on *might* be interested in him! Not to mention that he now had to ride the subway home wearing garbage bags and newspapers. How could things get any crazier?

And then Peter remembered: he had a science test coming up at the end of the week.

CHAPTER 6

Peter spent the next morning listening to Aunt May worry about Super Heroes in general and Spider-Man in particular.

"That Spider-Man really gets to me. I mean, why wear a mask if you don't have something to hide?" she asked.

Peter nearly smiled. Of course he wore his mask as Spider-Man in part so his enemies wouldn't harm the people he loved—to protect Aunt May—and here she was thinking he wore it to hide deep dark secrets about his intentions.

If she only knew . . .

When he got to school about an hour later, he found the usual mixed bag of talk: sports, music, celebrities, fellow students, and, of course, Spider-Man.

"DID YOU SEE THOSE CLIPS OF THE STOCK EXCHANGE?" Flash was asking one of his pals.

Peter rolled his eyes. Why did his locker have to be right next to Flash's?

"Man, not sure how Spider-Man does it, but he nails every crook in town."

Without thinking Peter jumped to his friend Nova's defense.

"NOVA'S NOT A **CROOK**,"

Peter fired back.

Flash turned around slowly.

"Figures he'd root for the villain," Flash said, right in Peter's face.

"What are you reading? The *Daily Bugle* Web site? Every other paper thinks Spider-Man saved the day," Flash stated.

PETEY HERE DOESN'T LIKE SPIDER-MAN SO MUCH.

"And I hate to do this, but I have to side with Flash here, Pete."

Peter turned around to see Gwen.

"My dad said himself that Spider-Man was a big help, even though he didn't give me details when I asked," she added.

"All I'm saying is I don't trust him, that's all," Peter said.

"And all I'm saying is you're just scared of

A LOT OF PEOPLE THINK SPIDER-MAN'S THE BAD GUY!

a *real* man like Spider-Man," Flash teased. "Afraid of what he'd do to a wimp like you? Huh?"

"FLASH, CUT IT OUT,"

Gwen said.

"Oh, sorry," Flash said as he threw his hands up. "Forgot you two geeks are in *love*."

"We're not . . ." Peter and Gwen said at the same time.

Flash biffed Peter on the head.

"Good choice, Parker. Her dad's a police officer. Maybe he can protect you from big, bad Spider-Man!" Flash said. "I'd watch my back when I'm walking to the subway if I were you. Look behind the shower curtain when you walk into the bathroom. Check under

your bed before you go to sleep. Spider-Man's coming for you. . . ." Flash said in a singsong voice.

"Ignore it, ignore it Peter whispered.

QUACK!

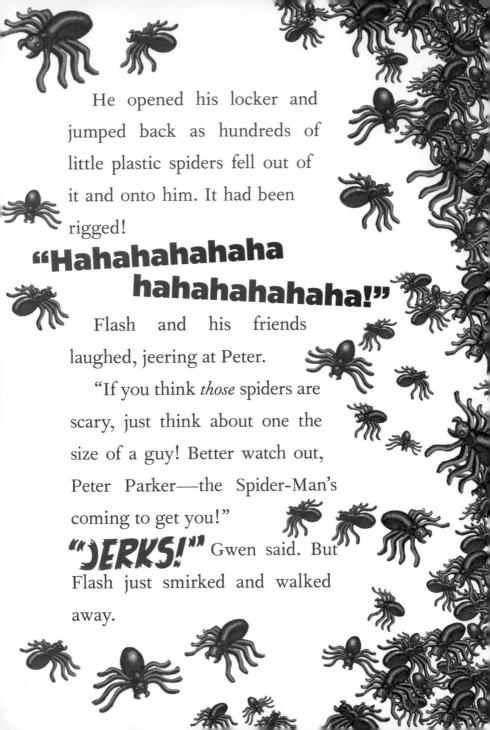

He opened his locker and jumped back as hundreds of little plastic spiders fell out of it and onto him. It had been rigged!

"Hahahahahaha hahahahahaha!"

Flash and his friends laughed, jeering at Peter.

"If you think *those* spiders are scary, just think about one the size of a guy! Better watch out, Peter Parker—the Spider-Man's coming to get you!"

"JERKS!" Gwen said. But Flash just smirked and walked away.

Gwen grabbed a few toy spiders. "Here, I'll help you clean these up," she said to Peter.

"Thanks," he said. "You know, I didn't really mean you weren't . . . that I wasn't . . . I mean, when Flash said that thing about me and you, I didn't want you to think . . ." Peter stuttered, scrambling for the right words.

"Oh, I know, don't worry about it. Neither did I. I mean, neither do I. Oh, never mind," Gwen said, brushing her hair behind an ear nervously. "Um, I'll see you in chemistry, yeah?"

"Er, yeah. See you in a bit," Peter said. He could feel his face getting all **warm**. It was a stranger feeling than anything else he'd ever felt.

It was even odder than his spider-sense.

CHAPTER 7

*T*hat night Peter decided he had to put everything else out of his mind and study. He knew high school was important if he wanted to have any shot at a good college and a career as a scientist. He powered on his tablet and started to read about chemistry, from things as simple as water's molecular structure to things as exciting as unbreakable metal alloys.

Peter had forgotten how much he loved

science. He had been so distracted by other things recently. He had totally lost sight of one of the things that made him happiest.

As he read and researched, he quickly dismissed the dozens of app updates and push notifications that popped up on his screen— everything from weather alerts to newly available game levels.

But one notice he dismissed too quickly. He was getting tired. He'd been studying for hours. He was sure he must have read it wrong. Because he could have sworn he had read something that couldn't be true.

Did that say what I thought it said? Peter wondered.

He tapped his search engine app and typed in *News for Spider-Man.*

DAILY BUGLE

NEWS ALERT!

SPIDER-MAN HELD BY THING OF FANTASTIC FOUR

By Tomas Palacios and Clarissa Wong
Reports of heroes turning bad have come in from all over the city. First it was Daredevil attacking Spider-Man at the Museum of Natural History. Then there was the "Human Rocket," Nova. Now it's the Fantastic Four's very own Thing, who released an online video confessing his plans to terrorize the five boroughs. In the video, Spider-Man could be seen tied to a chair, being held captive by the bulky brawler.

SPIDER-MAN CAUGHT IN
HERO'S WEB

By Jennifer Redding

What's happened to Spidey? That's the question on everyone's mind. . . .

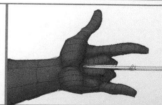

WHICH HERO IS NEXT TO TURN TO THE
DARK SIDE?

By Ron Lim

Captain America? Thor? Wolverine? These are some of the names being thrown around the Internet these days. . . .

Peter chose the *Daily Bugle*'s Web site. He knew that the publisher, a man named J. Jonah Jameson, hated Spider-Man. Jameson was convinced the hero was a menace, as he called him. And he spent most of his time trying to get the public to believe Spider-Man was a villain, too. But Jameson also had the best reporters in the business. So even though he forced his staff to paint Spider-Man in a bad light, the stories usually had more information than any other news source.

Peter tapped on a link to a video. He couldn't believe what he was seeing! The big, rocky Super Hero known as the Thing was standing in a dark room with what looked like Spider-Man tied to a chair in front of him.

"WHAT THE HECK?"

Peter said.

Peter pressed play. The clip began to run.

"IF YA HAVEN'T NOTICED, A BUNCH OF US ARE TIRED OF PLAYING THE PART OF THE SUPER HERO. WE WORK NIGHT AN' DAY PROTECTING YOU PEOPLE, AND WE GET NOTHING OUT OF IT," the Thing said. "SO WE'RE GONNA TAKE WHAT YOU OWE US, WITHOUT ASKING. CONSIDER IT PAYBACK. DAREDEVIL IS ON BOARD WITH US, AND SO IS NOVA. AND EVERY DAY MORE AN' MORE STEP FORWARD. THEY WANT TO JOIN THE SUPER HERO RESISTANCE.

"BUT THIS BOZO OVER HERE HASN'T DONE ANYTHING BUT GET IN OUR WAY."

"AND BECAUSE OF THAT," the Thing

continued, as he SLAPPED his captive Spider-Man upside the head.

Whoa! Peter flinched. Even a love tap from the Thing would hurt! he thought.

The Thing went on, "WE'RE GOING TO MAKE HIM HELP US. IN FACT, WE'RE GONNA KEEP HIM LOCKED UP IN HERE TO DO OUR DIRTY WORK. OUR REAL DIRTY WORK, THAT IS—CLEANING THE TOILETS, IRONING OUR COSTUMES, WHATEVER."

It was weird for Peter to see himself on-screen in that position, even though he knew the guy on the screen wasn't *really* Spider-Man.

"SEE, YOU GOT TWENTY-FOUR HOURS. IF YOU HAND OVER THE LAPTOP THIS GUY OVER HERE SNAGGED FROM US, WE'LL SET SPIDER-MAN FREE. OTHERWISE, WE SQUASH HIM LIKE THE

BUG HE IS, AND ME AND NOVA AND DAREDEVIL AND A WHOLE BUNCH OF OTHER HEROES DESTROY THE CITY, ONE BOROUGH AT A TIME. AND WE TAKE THE SPOILS FOR OURSELVES.

"AND JUST IN CASE YOU PEOPLE DON'T CARE IF SPIDER-MAN LIVES OR DIES, I HAVE A SPECIAL TREAT FOR YOU. I'M GONNA UNMASK THIS GUY. EVEN IF SPIDER-MAN DOESN'T HAVE ANY FRIENDS OR FAMILY, THE GUY UNDER THE MASK PROBABLY DOES. THAT MEANS SOMEONE'S BOUND TO STEP UP."

Peter leaned in. This was getting weirder and weirder.

The Thing's big rocky hand clenched the mask of the Spider-Man on the screen. The Thing whipped it off and revealed the wall-crawler's true identity. **Spider-Man was really . . .**

FLASH THOMPSON?

CHAPTER

8

"**W**hoa," was all Peter could utter.

He stared at the screen. How in the world had Flash Thompson wound up in this situation? And where had he gotten that cheesy Spidey suit? I mean, mine looks waaay better

than that, Peter thought. None of this was making sense. Was it all just a trap? Was Flash in on it?

Someone knocked on Peter's bedroom door.

"Come in," Peter said, and Aunt May entered.

"Peter, there was just a report on the TV," she said, sounding very nervous. "A boy from your school's been kidnapped. A boy named **EUGENE**. They're saying he might be Spider-Man!"

"I know, I saw," Peter said.

"Well, please, *please* be careful, Peter. Shut and lock that window," she said while shutting and locking it herself. "These Super Heroes can **fly**, they can blast through walls—sometimes it seems there's nothing they can't do."

"In that case I'm not sure how much a locked window's going to do," Peter chuckled.

She took his hand. "I couldn't bear if something were to happen to you."

Peter kissed her on the cheek.

"I CAN TAKE CARE OF MYSELF," he said. And although Aunt May smiled and nodded, Peter could tell by the look on her face that she didn't believe him.

"I've got some homework to finish up," he sighed. "Don't worry about it, Aunt May. We'll be all right. Who's going to come looking for a random lady and her nephew in the middle of Queens? I mean, what would they get out of it? Unless they're looking for your choco-late-chip cookies. I can see that, actually. They're worthy of an attack on the house!"

This managed to get a chuckle from Aunt May, who closed the door as she left the room, wishing Peter luck in his studies.

But Peter wasn't laughing at all, and he definitely wasn't thinking about his studies. As soon as he was alone, he started to research more about the story. According to what he read, no one knew where the clip had been

Belvedere Castle

filmed. The **DAILY BUGLE** site said that the Thing had contacted it saying he and the other fallen Super Heroes wanted the laptop dropped off at Belvedere Castle in Central Park. Police had already roped off and searched that area and found no sign of the Thing, Spider-Man, or anyone else.

Peter paused. It didn't *really* sound like Flash's life was in danger. The Thing had basically said they were going to turn Flash into their housekeeper. He'd have a miserable life. He'd spend every minute worried that the heroes were waiting around every corner, ready to toss orders at him. He'd be afraid to simply walk down a hall. Basically, he'd feel the same way he made Peter feel every day at school.

Maybe Spider-Man didn't need to get involved in this one. After all, it looked like the cops had it under control.

And if they didn't, wouldn't Flash just be getting what he deserved?

Peter turned off his tablet, lay down on his bed, and stared at the ceiling. He was imagining his new, easy life at school without Flash.

He thought about it a lot.

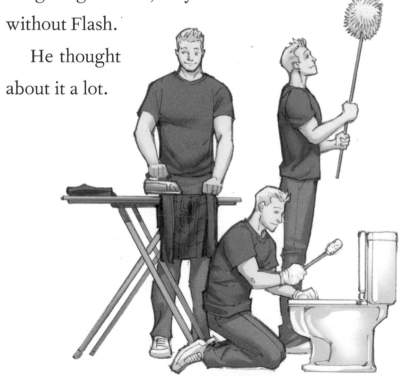

And after a long while of thinking about it, when Aunt May was asleep and the house was quiet, Peter put on his Spider-Man costume. He leaped from his window and swung toward New York City. As much as Peter disliked Flash Thompson, Spider-Man needed to save the day.

CHAPTER

*I*n no time, Spider-Man had swung over the bridge and straight to Central Park. He carried an old, broken laptop tucked away in his costume. He'd dug it out of his closet and stripped it, knowing he could always use the spare parts for his tech experiments. Then he had taken the shell of the machine with him to Central Park.

He saw Belvedere Castle in the distance. It

was a huge building made to look like a grand palace. It overlooked a quiet pond and sat next to the park's Great Lawn. Best of all, it was surrounded by trees. This made it easy for Spider-Man to sneak past the police. He climbed into the treetops and made a web tightrope from one to another, walking over the heads of officers who were guarding the castle. When he reached a group

of trees that over-
looked the palace,
he shot a web
toward its tower
and swung down
to the courtyard
where the *Bugle*'s
article said the Thing
wanted the laptop left.
Right after Spider-Man
dropped it off, he swung back up
into the trees, completely unseen.

Then he waited in the trees.

NOTHING.

Spider-Man had hoped that whoever was behind this had been watching the castle. He thought they'd show themselves when he dropped the laptop off, but no luck. The police barricade must have kept the place clear. Spider-Man needed to move to Plan B. He took out his phone and zoomed in on the castle courtyard and the computer and began recording.

"I've delivered the laptop, as you've requested. Now, set Spider-Man free," he said in a voice much deeper than his own. Then he created a fake name, uploaded the video to VidTube, and sent an e-mail to every media outlet he could think of.

In just a matter of minutes, he noticed the police starting to move in. But before they even got close to the castle, Spider-Man heard a roar overhead. He looked up and saw something shooting across the sky. It sounded like a jet's roar, but it was moving way too fast.

The streak shot down to the courtyard, near where the laptop was, and then darted right back up into the sky. Spider-Man knew he was about to lose the laptop and whoever had taken it. Worse still, he had a feeling that they weren't going to keep up their part of the deal and return Flash Thompson.

Spider-Man needed to act, and fast. As the streak of red and gold whizzed overhead, Spidey shot a web at the heels of the flying figure and was soon jerked up. He was whisked away, over the park and New York City, riding behind the criminal like a windsurfer. He held on tightly to the webs as he soared over the skyline at what felt like light speed.

He guessed that whoever he was following hadn't felt the webs attach to him and had no idea Spider-Man had hitched a ride. Skyscrapers and bridges seemed to zoom by. The water below was calm, but surely cold this time of year. As they started to descend, Spider-Man worried they were going to land right in it.

But upon hitting the ground, he discovered they'd landed on one of the many small islands that surrounded the city—the ones that were off limits to almost everyone and hardly ever occupied.

Spider-Man looked up, and looking directly back at him was

IRON MAN!

"You've gone bad, too, huh?"
Spider-Man said.

He expected Iron Man to raise up his hands and blast him with one of his repulsor beams. But he just tried to run—and in a pretty clunky way, at that.

"Um, you're not actually Iron Man, are you?" Spider-Man said to whomever was limping away from him. One thing was sure—the guy trying to pass for Iron Man wasn't doing such a great job of it.

Spider-Man shot his webs at the fleeing suspect. The bad guy quickly got tangled up and fell down. Spidey ran up to him and noticed that he was wearing a good—but not nearly perfect—replica of one of Iron Man's suits of armor. He tore off the man's helmet and gasped. He was face-to-face with a hairless man whose pale skin was so white he could practically see his veins beneath.

"Where's Flash?" Spider-Man asked.

The villain laughed, as if to say he wasn't going to tell him.

Spider-Man looked around. The island was very small. It could fit no more than a few houses on it. He spotted a crude shack on the opposite shore. He rushed there and tore off the splintered door.

And there he was: Flash Thompson. He was tied to a chair, still wearing the Spider-Man costume without his mask. And he looked desperate and terrified, and most bizarrely for Peter, he was hysterically crying.

Spider-Man rushed over to untie him.

"It's okay, kid. We're going to get you out of here," he told him.

As he loosened the ropes to free Flash, Spider-Man noticed that the high school student was shaking, almost violently. He was too scared even to stand. Spider-Man steadied Flash as he continued to sob.

"I'm so sorry. It was so stupid of me. So, so stupid!" Flash cried.

"Look, this wasn't your fault,"

Spider-Man said, amazed at himself for feeling bad for Flash.

"But it—it sort of was. There's this kid at school. And he's real scared of you. I thought it was funny, so I . . ."

"You put on a Spider-Man costume to scare him," Spider-Man finished, and Flash nodded.

"You're right, that was stupid," Spider-Man admitted as he whipped away the last rope from Flash's hands. "But not stupid enough to wind up in this position."

"He—he thought I was you," Flash finished. "I was hiding behind the basketball courts and he must have seen me there. He thought I was you and . . ."

Flash began to cry again.

Spider-Man's spider-sense tingled and he turned, expecting the guy he'd webbed up to be behind him. But then he realized that his senses were reacting to something *below*.

He pushed Flash and the chair out of the way and made a fist.

"WELL, IT TOOK YOU LONG ENOUGH, WEBHEAD!" said the Thing from the bottom

of a pit that had to be at least a hundred feet deep. Thing was joined by Daredevil, Nova, and Iron Man.

"This is odd," Spider-Man asked.

"Just get us outta here and we'll explain everything," Nova said.

Spider-Man spun a webbed ladder into the pit and slowly the heroes emerged. A few times it looked like the huge Thing might not make it, but he eventually clawed his way up.

Spider-Man told them he'd tied up the guy responsible for this outside.

"LEMME AT 'IM," the Thing said as he stormed out of the shack and the other heroes and Flash followed.

The others explained that the guy who'd captured them called himself the **Chameleon**. He was a master of disguise. He was able to change his skin to look like anyone, or anything. And he could do the same with his clothes, which also responded to his thoughts.

"He could even make clothes that helped him fly?" Spider-Man asked, remembering how **Cha eleon** had posed as Nova and Iron Man and flown away.

"Nah, those were some second-rate jet packs," Iron Man said, pointing to the back of the **Cha eleon**'s Iron Man suit. The real Iron Man kicked it and it crumbled apart.

"So that's why he couldn't fire a repulsor blast," Spider-Man realized. "And why his Nova blast was so weak."

Spider-Man learned that each of the heroes had been trapped the same way. The **Cha eleon** had posed as a fellow hero and led them to the deserted island. Once there he'd told them that there was trouble down an abandoned tunnel, at the other end of the island. Once the heroes were at the far end of the tunnel the **Cha eleon** slammed down

Vibranium walls and trapped the heroes inside, then took on their identities.

"That's why he wanted the **VIBRANIUM** from the museum," Spidey realized. "A little bit of it goes a long way. He could have used even that little chunk of it to reinforce the tunnel."

"He should have thought of that earlier," Nova noted. "The Thing was able to dig through the tunnel floor. I helped burrow through the ground and Daredevil's senses helped us navigate the network of tunnels under this place. We heard the commotion at this end of the island and headed over. That's when you found us."

"JUST TA MAKE SURE, WHY DON'T YA DO SOMETHING TO PROVE YOU ACTUALLY ARE SPIDER-MAN?" the Thing demanded.

"Ta-da,"

Spider-Man said as he landed.

"Who's this guy, then?" Iron Man asked, pointing to Flash.

"Oh, him?"

Spider-Man asked, looking over at Flash. "He's just a kid who's learning that playing games isn't always so much fun."

CHAPTER

*L*ed by the Thing, the other heroes took the Chameleon to the authorities, and Flash Thompson back home. Spider-Man raced back to his own home in Queens.

After all, he had homework to finish up.

The next day Midtown High was abuzz with the news. As he

walked down the hall, Peter caught bits of conversation. It was always strange for him to hear some of the things people had to say about Spider-Man's adventures.

"FLASH IS SPIDER-MAN'S BACKUP NOW."

"THE X-MEN WERE BEHIND IT ALL."

"SPIDER-MAN WAS WORKING WITH THE CROOKS!"

By his locker, Peter noticed a group of kids gathered around. As he pushed through the mob, he saw Flash in the middle. He was smiling and laughing and talking to the group.

"Scared? No way, dude, I wasn't scared!" he was saying to a kid standing next to him. "I actually think the Chameleon was scared of *me*! Sure, I played it cool at first, but after he turned off that camera, I got tough. 'Listen,' I said, 'I've got a lot of powerful friends. They'll be looking for me.' And then, of course, Spidey—that's what I call him, 'Spidey'—swooped in to help me out. And together we put the Chameleon away. You know I think Spider-Man is freaking amazing, but even he needs a hand sometimes. I was happy to lend him one."

Peter couldn't help laughing as he walked by, hearing all this. He glanced at Flash and caught his eye. The two of them looked at each other for a second. Then Peter pushed through the rest of the crowd and moved on to his locker.

"I mean, that guy never stood a chance," Flash said. "Between me and Spider-Man— man, he didn't know what he was getting himself into. . . ."

"HEY, PETE!"

Peter turned around to find Gwen. "Crazy what's going on here, huh? I'm just glad Flash is okay. I mean, the guy can be a jerk, but still . . ."

Peter looked at her and smiled.

"Yeah, I guess I know what you mean," he said.

"So, you ready for the test?" Gwen asked, and Peter shrugged, not really sure. He had been studying late into the night.

The morning bell rang. Peter removed his

books and closed his locker. Then he moved through the thinning crowd and walked with Gwen to their first class.

Peter looked back at Flash, who was high-fiving kids as they walked away.

"You'd think he'd learn a thing or two. You know, after being kidnapped by a Super Villain and all," Peter said.

"What makes you so sure he hasn't?" Gwen asked.

"I don't know. I just wouldn't count on it," Peter said, remembering how different the scared and shaking Flash was from the one who was celebrating in the hallway.

As they continued to walk to class, Peter heard someone call his name. Then the person called it again.

"HEY, PARKER!"

Flash shouted out to him from down the hall.

Peter took a deep breath and turned around slowly.

Flash was running toward him. It looked like he had something in his hand. Peter braced himself to block whatever was about to be thrown at him.

"YOU DROPPED THIS OUT OF YOUR LOCKER,"

Flash said, holding out a crumpled piece of paper.

Peter opened it and was surprised and confused by what he saw. He wasn't sure what to say. So he said the natural thing.

"Thanks, Flash."

"Yep, you bet," Flash said. Then he jogged back down the hall to catch up with his friends, who were moving on to whatever they had next on their schedules.

Gwen shot Peter a smile.

"YOU WERE SAYING?"

she asked.

Peter smiled back, happy that for once he wasn't the only one trying to hide a deep, dark secret. And that maybe, just maybe, Spider-Man had helped somebody change. Even if it was just a little bit.

For Stella and Vivian,
my little Super Heroes! –MS

STARRING

CAPTAIN AMERICA

BY MICHAEL SIGLAIN

ILLUSTRATED BY

RON LIM AND ANDY TROY

Los Angeles
New York

FEATURING YOUR FAVORITES!

The First Avenger!

CAPTAIN AMERICA

Alias

STEVE ROGERS

FALCON

COULSON

Director of S.H.I.E.L.D.

NICK FURY

BLACK WIDOW

IRON MAN

Alias

TONY STARK

ARNIM ZOLA

HYDRA-PRIME

HYDRA

I love New York!

STATUE OF LIBERTY

CUP OF JOE

Steve's coffee guy

OLD JOE

COOL MOTORCYCLE

Made of Vibranium!

CAP'S SHIELD

THE STORY OF CAPTAIN AMERICA

*A*ll Steve Rogers ever wanted was to join the army. But he was frail and weak and unable to enlist. Then Steve was chosen to take part in a top secret experiment called **Project: Rebirth.** He was given the Super-Soldier Serum and was bathed in pulsating Vita-Rays.

When the experiment was over, Steve had been transformed from a small and thin weakling into a big, tall, and strong Super-Soldier.

Steve was given a special uniform and an unbreakable red, white, and blue shield made from a rare metal called Vibranium. He promised to fight for freedom and equality for all as

CAPTAIN AMERICA!

After one particularly tough battle with the evil villain called Red Skull, Cap's plane crashed into the icy waters of the Arctic. The plane—with Cap still inside—was frozen for many decades, until it was discovered by S.H.I.E.L.D., the world's best super spies. They soon revived Captain America from his icy slumber.

Steve joined S.H.I.E.L.D.'s team of Super Heroes, known as the Avengers. Now, fighting alongside Iron Man, Hulk, Black Widow, Hawkeye, and Falcon, Captain America once again defends liberty and justice from evildoers everywhere!

CHAPTER 1

Steve Rogers woke up at 4:55 a.m., minutes before his alarm clock rang. He jumped out of bed, stretched, and began his morning routine. By 5:15, Steve had already done 3,250 push-ups and 4,500 sit-ups, and he hadn't *even broken a sweat.*

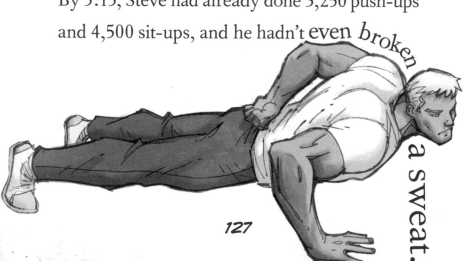

Next it was time for his morning jog— a quick ten-mile run around the streets of **NEW YORK CITY**.

Steve left his apartment, breathed in the warm June air, and began his jog. Good runners could finish a mile in five minutes. Steve could do it in under two.

Steve made his way downtown and to forty-Second Street, then cut over to Broadway. As he ran, Steve looked up at the giant billboards and bright lights of Times Square. Steve definitely preferred the old Big Apple.

Steve ended his run downtown in front of a newsstand and was instantly greeted with a **"HIYA, CAP"** from the guy working the stand, whom everyone called Old Joe.

"JUST STEVE, PLEASE," Steve said.

"The usual?" Old Joe called out. Steve nodded, and the man handed him *the* **DAILY BUGLE**. Steve still couldn't believe a newspaper cost a dollar. He remembered when they were just five cents!

"Glad you're still buying the paper," Old Joe began. "You're my best customer. Most people today get their news from phones or computers. You even pay with actual money. It's like the 1940s all over again," he said with a smile.

Steve smiled back, took the paper, and walked across the street to get a cup of coffee. Usually, he'd go to the local **DINER**.

But after hearing Old Joe talk about the '40s and how different things were today, Steve thought he would try something new, so he made his way to the trendy coffee shop down the block.

The shop was buzzing with people. They barely stopped moving long enough to order their drinks, all of which sounded weird to Steve. He stared at the chalkboard menu.

When it was his turn, Steve asked for "just a cup of joe," and the kid behind the counter stared back at him blankly.

"You want what?" the server asked, confused.

"A CUP OF JOE, BLACK," Steve replied, but there was still no response. "You do sell coffee here, right?" Steve asked. The kid was amazed that someone wanted just a regular black coffee with nothing else in it. Steve paid for his overpriced drink, then took his paper and sat on a bench outside.

So much for trying something different, he thought.

Steve looked around and sighed. People were walking with their heads down, busy with other things,

oblivious to the world around them. Everyone was
connected to technology, but not . . . .
. . . .
. . . .
. . . . to

one another. In Steve's day, people talked to
each other. They read and conversed rather than
losing themselves in their own virtual worlds.

But before he could continue thinking about how different things were, a strong voice called out to him. **"CAPTAIN, WE HAVE A SITUATION . . ."** the voice began. Steve looked up to see his Avengers teammate Sam Wilson, code name **FALCON**, standing before him. Steve instantly rose to his feet.

"What's the mission?" Steve asked, ready to jump into battle.

IT'S A MATTER OF EXTREME URGENCY!

Sam began. "I've got an extra ticket to today's Yankees game and no one to go with me. What do you say? Want to take in America's favorite pastime?" he asked.

Steve smiled. It wasn't an actual mission, but a baseball game with Sam would still be fun.

"Count me in," Steve said. "Besides, I haven't been to a ball game since Joltin' Joe played."

"JOLTIN' WHO?" Sam asked as they walked back uptown.

"Never mind," Steve said with a sigh. Little did he know that day would be the start of the most dangerous mission of Cap's career.

CHAPTER 2

Captain America and Falcon stood before Nick Fury, the director of the super-spy group known as S.H.I.E.L.D. Cap—in his **RED**, *WHITE*, and **BLUE** uniform— was a very impressive figure. Next to him was Falcon, wearing a high-tech flight suit that, when activated, allowed him to **FLY** with holographic wings. Both heroes stood at attention on board S.H.I.E.L.D.'s massive

Helicarrier—part aircraft carrier, part helicopter, and all state of the art. The ability of this futuristic vessel to fly unseen above Manhattan still impressed Steve.

"Gentlemen," the eye-patch-wearing Fury began as he called up a digital HUD. "Within the last three weeks, reports of missing persons around the tristate area have more than tripled. Men and women, all between the ages of eighteen and thirty, all seemingly in perfect health and in top physical condition."

"Think they're all connected?" Cap asked.

LOCAL LAW ENFORCEMENT DOESN'T, BUT I DO.

"Stay alert," Fury said. "The kidnappings seem to be random, but **S.H.I.E.L.D.** intelligence tells me that there's something bigger going on. I have several agents hard at work trying to figure out who is behind this, and why."

"What's our involvement?" Falcon asked.

"Right now, observe and report only. I want you up to speed for when we need to act," Fury said.

As Cap and Falcon walked out of Fury's office, the First Avenger felt disappointed.

He was looking forward to some action, not sitting on the sidelines. But before he could harp

on the issue too long, Falcon gave him a nudge.

"Come on, Cap," Falcon said. "We're going to be late for the game. The Helicarrier is going up the East Coast and will be over the Bronx in two minutes—just enough time for us to change into less conspicuous clothing."

Steve Rogers walked around Yankee Stadium in shock. There was music blasting, a huge TV, dozens of smaller TVs, various fancy restaurants and food stands, and even clothing shops.

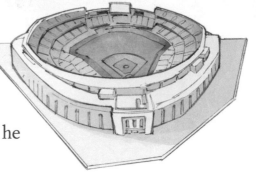

"This certainly isn't the House that Ruth Built," he said to Sam.

"You're living in another time, man. Welcome to the twenty-first century, where everything is at your fingertips!" Sam said.

As they sat, Steve wondered why a music video kept playing on the jumbotron screen. "Oh, that's one of the outfielders," Sam said. "He has the number-three song in the country."

"Babe Ruth and Joe DiMaggio never sang," Steve said under his breath. "Isn't anyone interested in the game anymore?"

But before Sam could respond, their

S.H.I.E.L.D. emergency beacons started to  **BLINK**. It was Fury. There was a team of college kids on the way to the game, but their bus had gone missing. S.H.I.E.L.D. intercepted the garbled 911 call, and Sam and Steve were being called in to respond.

They ran out of the stadium and stood before Steve's **vintage 1942 Harley-Davidson motorcycle.** "You can't be serious," Sam said, referring to the battered and bruised cycle. "You could walk faster than that thing goes." But Steve was already opening a large duffel bag to reveal his Captain America uniform and Vibranium shield.

"She hasn't failed me yet," Cap said with a smile. "Now suit up and hop on."

"No way. I can fly. I'll carry you," Sam responded as his holographic hard-light wings began to form.

"Not a chance," Steve said as he lowered his mask into position. He jumped on his bike and started it with a loud roar. **Now _THIS_ was Cap's favorite pastime!**

CHAPTER 3

Falcon shook his head, then took to the air and activated the GPS on his watch. "I've got a lock on them, so try to keep up!" Falcon said as he flew toward the Major Deegan Expressway. Captain America followed on his bike, darting *IN* and *OUT* of traffic until he spotted the hijacked school bus.

Cap sped past all the other cars until he was

right behind the bus. Suddenly, the emergency doors at the back of the bus burst open.

Energy beams shot from the windows. Whoever these guys were, they were very heavily armed.

FALCON! I COULD USE A DIVERSION!

"**UNDERSTOOD**,"

Falcon said. The flying hero dove down and fired a grappling hook at the roof of the bus, penetrating the thick top. Falcon swung high into the air and yanked with all his might, causing the driver to swerve. The distraction worked! Cap sped up and drove out of harm's way.

Inside the bus, an armed goon attached a small device to the end of the grappling hook and sent an electric charge up the wire and straight back to Falcon. It **SHOCKED** the hero, and Falcon fell to the ground. The villain laughed as the bus sped away. "We did it," the goon said. "Inform headquarters that the test subjects will be there within the hour."

The Goon

But before the driver could respond, he pointed out the window; the armed goon followed his gaze. "No! It can't be," the driver said in disbelief. The villains saw him from a distance, standing atop an overpass, looking directly at them: it was Captain America!

Cap jumped on his bike and revved the engine, but it sputtered out. "Not now!" Cap said under his breath. He tried his bike again. **Nothing!**

The bus was getting closer and closer. He tried a third time. The bike sputtered again and then conked out.

The motorcycle that had never failed . . . failed. By then the bus was almost under the overpass. There was only one thing to do. Captain America ran at full speed and

JUMPED!

The bus swerved left and right, then burst through a guardrail and came to a stop.

Cap, who had been clinging to the top of the bus, quickly jumped to his feet and swung down through one of the side windows.

"Ah, the great Captain America," the villain said as he raised his weapon.

The goon fired, but Cap was too fast. The beams **bounced** off his raised shield. Then Cap *THREW* his shield! The

DOOM!"

hostages stood there, stunned, as the goon fell to the ground. Then Cap noticed that the driver had gotten away.

"Wait here," he instructed the hostages. "I'll be right back!"

Captain America jumped off the bus and ran at top speed toward the driver. The driver had pulled out a high-tech energy weapon, ready to fire, when—

WHAM!

Falcon smashed down on the villain and **KNOCKED HIM OUT COLD.**

"Who are these guys?" Falcon asked.

"I don't know, but they're too heavily armed for a hostage situation," Cap said. "Fury's right: there's more to this than meets the eye. And I don't like it."

"Captain America? Falcon?" a voice called from behind them. "We'll take it from here." It was Agent Coulson from **S.H.I.E.L.D.** He and his team were ushering the hostages off the bus and taking the villains into custody. "Please report to Director Fury's office at oh seven hundred tomorrow morning," Coulson said. Then he wheeled Cap's bike up to him. "Think you might want to requisition a new ride, Captain," Coulson quipped.

"No, thanks," Cap said as he quickly took the bike from him and wheeled it off toward the **S.H.I.E.L.D.** trucks.

"Was it something I said?" Coulson asked Falcon.

"Nah, he's just upset. He almost jeopardized the hostages thanks to his old motorcycle."

Cap heard what Falcon said. **And he was right.**

CHAPTER

4

*A*t seven the next morning, Steve Rogers stood in his civilian clothing before Director Fury.

THANKS FOR COMING IN, CAP. PLEASE SIT DOWN. SAM WILL JOIN US LATER. FIRST, WE NEED TO TALK.

YOU WERE RIGHT. THAT WASN'T A NORMAL KIDNAPPING ATTEMPT.

"Coulson will deal with what happened yesterday," Fury said before changing the subject. "Your help is needed elsewhere." He pressed a button under his desk.

The windows went black as a flat-screen TV lowered itself from the ceiling. "Watch this, and then we'll talk," Fury said as he pressed another button.

Steve watched the screen as the men in the video spoke in hushed tones. "Notice anything special about those men?" Fury asked. Steve studied the video more closely.

"There are six of them, but . . . but only two of them look. . .real," Steve said, almost in disbelief.

"Good eye. The other four are advanced holograms. But keep watching," Fury said.

"*EVERYTHING IS PROCEEDING ACCORD-
ING TO SCHEDULE. THE TECHNO-DISRUPTOR
HAS BEEN COMPLETED AND THE TOMORROW
ARMY WILL SOON BE READY*," said one of the
holograms.

"*EXCELLENT. THE FINAL MEETING IS SET
FOR MIDNIGHT TOMORROW AT GRAVESEND
BAY*," said one of the non-holograms. "*I WILL
INFORM OUR LEADER*." And with that, the

video abruptly ended and the light in the office returned. Steve turned toward Fury.

"What is the Tomorrow Army?" Steve asked. "And where did this video come from?"

Fury pressed another button; a few seconds later, the beautiful yet dangerous Natasha Romanoff, code name Black Widow, entered the room.

"I took the video, and it wasn't easy," Natasha said, then explained how she'd had to hold herself up in the rafters. "After the video cut out and the holograms disappeared, the two men raised both their arms and said:

HAIL, HYDRA!

Steve's fists clenched at the mere mention of **HYDRA**, an evil organization that wanted to take over the world. They were the very opposite of the super spies who made up **S.H.I.E.L.D.** and worked to keep the world safe.

"I followed them down a hidden elevator shaft and tailed them to a secret underground training room. There were dozens of guards—all training with different weapons or in different fighting styles. . . .and all wearing **HYDRA** badges," Natasha said.

"It's not possible," Steve said. "**HYDRA** was defeated almost

a century ago—by me!"
"That's what we thought,"
Fury said. "Then we
found this."

He handed Cap an envelope marked
TOP SECRET. "Twelve of my best
agents ended up in the hospital getting us this
info," Fury said. Cap opened the envelope to
find several glossy pictures. "I think you'll
recognize the person in the center of the room."

Steve's eyes widened, and his blood ran
COLD. "No . . ." Steve whispered. The figure in the picture was a hulking one. It had a
large half-human, half-robotic body—but its
face wasn't on its head. Instead, it was on a tele-
vision-like flat screen in the center of its body.
The body was unrecognizable, but the face

was unmistakable. It was **HYDRA** scientist and second-in-command Arnim Zola. Like Steve, Zola had fought in World War II. But Steve had thought Zola long dead.

In the photos, Zola was standing in front of a high-tech machine straight out of a science-fiction movie. "Somehow, Arnim Zola survived all these years and is now the head of Hydra," Fury said. "We believe that the thing he's standing in front of is the Techno-Disruptor." Then Fury turned to face Steve, who had already suited up and was ready for battle.

YOUR MISSION IS TO CAPTURE ZOLA AND STOP HYDRA—ONCE AND FOR ALL.

When Cap went to grab his shield, he noticed a new black-and-gray uniform that hung next to it. "That's your new stealth suit," a voice behind him said. It was Nick Fury again. "It will allow you to sneak into the **HYDRA** meeting place without being detected," the director said. "It's a present from Tony Stark. He's making them for all the **AVENGERS**.

"I know you prefer **red, white,** and **blue**—but this will keep you from being caught and becoming **black** and **blue,"** Fury said with a grin.

As Fury left, Cap suited up again and made his way into **S.H.I.E.L.D.'s** equipment room.

Agent Coulson approached Cap with Cap's bike. "You know, we can add a rocket launcher, a GPS, even a cup holder to this thing," Coulson began, but Cap refused. This was

WHOOSH!

a classic bike, after all, and didn't want to change it. "I once felt the same way about Lola," Coulson said as he got into his classic red Corvette.

He flipped a switch. And with that, Coulson and Lola rocketed toward New York City below.

Cap shook his head at the flying car as Falcon and Black Widow stepped up behind him.

"I just heard the news about HYDRA," Sam said. "When do we go after them?"

"We don't. I do," Cap replied.

"Let me help!" Sam responded. But Cap refused. He was going in solo to find out more about HYDRA'S secret plans, and he didn't need help. HYDRA was a dangerous and evil organization from Steve's past, and he knew exactly how to handle it.

But Cap wanted to be extra careful, especially when it came to his friends.

Sam walked off, frustrated that he couldn't help, but Natasha stayed behind to have a word with Steve.

SPYING ON HYDRA ALONE, AND ON THIS RICKETY OLD BIKE, REALLY ISN'T SMART. I SHOULD DO THIS MISSION.

I'VE GOT THE SITUATION UNDER CONTROL.

I'M SURE YOU DO—BUT TAKE THIS WITH YOU.

It was an emergency signal. If Cap was over whelmed, he'd tap the screen and **S.H.I.E.L.D.** would be there.

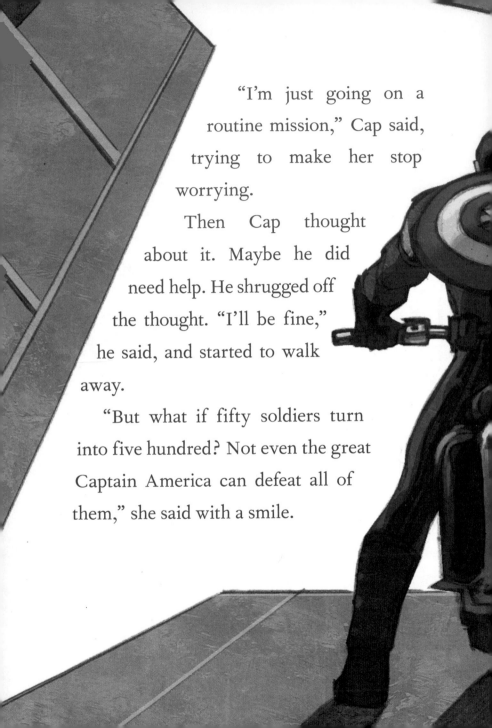

"I'm just going on a routine mission," Cap said, trying to make her stop worrying.

Then Cap thought about it. Maybe he did need help. He shrugged off the thought. "I'll be fine," he said, and started to walk away.

"But what if fifty soldiers turn into five hundred? Not even the great Captain America can defeat all of them," she said with a smile.

"Then I'm going to need a lot more than this beacon," Cap replied. He strapped on a parachute, got on his bike, and prepared to ride off the ramp.

"Hey, Cap," Black Widow said as he started the engine. **"Be careful."** Cap nodded, then gunned his bike and rode straight off the ramp and into the open air high above **New York City.**

Once he landed, Cap revved the engine and sped out of sight, toward the Brooklyn docks.

The thought that this venomous group was back made Cap's blood boil. It was time to take the fight to

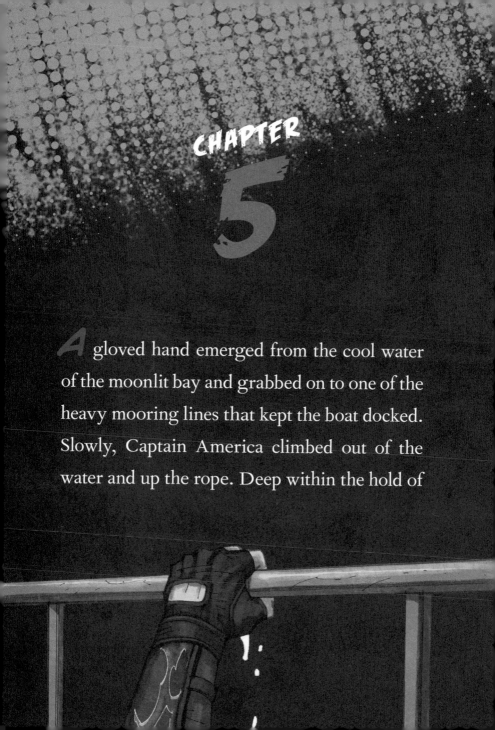

5

A gloved hand emerged from the cool water of the moonlit bay and grabbed on to one of the heavy mooring lines that kept the boat docked. Slowly, Captain America climbed out of the water and up the rope. Deep within the hold of the boat was a high-tech *HYDRA* meeting room, and Cap was going to find it.

He quietly made his way across the deck, taking out one *HYDRA* guard after another.

Cap's new uniform was a great help. The black-and-gray suit allowed him to blend with shadows and move without being seen.

Cap quickly took out a big guard with his trusty shield. He left the unconscious guard locked in a storage room but without his helmet and armor. Cap, now disguised as a

HYDRA guard, made his way to the bottom of the boat and into the secret meeting room. He stood silently in the back. At the center of the room was something—or someone. It was standing upright and was surrounded by a dozen HYDRA scientists, all of whom had evil smiles on their evil faces. They spoke of special gauntlets and boots that could increase a man's **STRENGTH** and *SPEED*; of high-tech armor and state-of-the-art helmets—helmets that were combat ready and could withstand a blast at point-blank range. Then they mentioned that this futuristic weaponry was ready to test today. Captain America had heard enough.

"Party's over, boys!" Cap said as he ripped off his *HYDRA* disguise and jumped into the center of the room. The guards fired their weapons immediately, but they were no match for Cap! Captain America raised his shield and blocked every attack, sending bullets and laser beams back toward the *HYDRA* agents, blasting them down and knocking them out.

"You are so right, Captain," one of the

HYDRA scientists began. "But for you!"

The scientist then pressed a code into a key-pad, and the metal box in the center of the room began to open with an eerie **HISSS.**

As the box opened, a high-tech **HYDRA** agent stepped out wearing the same devices that the other agents had been speaking about earlier. The super **HYDRA** goon clenched his fists, smirked, and took a step toward Cap.

The super-agent raised his gauntlets and brought them crashing down on Cap with ease. Cap lifted his shield at the last possible second to block the blow, but the shock wave went right through him and rattled his bones. *Wow,* Cap thought. *Felt like Thor bashed me with Mjolnir.* Before Cap knew it, the super-agent was on the ATTACK!

Cap dodged a punch, but then the super-agent grabbed him by the shoulder and unleashed an intense electroshock.

Cap screamed in pain and pushed forward, delivering a massive right hook to the agent's jaw that caused him to release Cap from his grip.

"You have a strong fighting spirit," the super-agent began. "But you are unwise to continue this fight. **You are no match for me.**"

"I'VE NEVER RUN FROM A FIGHT, AND I'M NOT ABOUT TO START NOW!"

Cap leaped into the air, but the **HYDRA** super-agent was too fast for him. He reared back and brought his fists **SLAMMING** down on Cap. Cap raised his shield again, but it was no use.

WHOOSH!

Cap landed with a hard **THUD** on the far side of the meeting room and momentarily blacked out. When he opened his eyes, Cap couldn't believe what had happened to his shield.

CAPTAIN AMERICA WAS IN TROUBLE.

He struggled to his feet as the super-agent charged toward him. Cap slowly raised his dented shield. But the super-agent was already looming above him.

The super-agent grabbed Cap's shield and flung it across the room—with Cap attached! Cap landed on his feet and quickly slung his shield across his back.

He moved in close and delivered a series of punches to no avail.

The super-agent looked down at Cap and grinned.

He then pressed a switch on his gauntlet and began to punch. And he punched and punched and punched—faster and faster and faster.

Then he sent another *SHOCK* through Cap's body that nearly *ZAPPED* him right out of his boots.

Cap fell to his knees, barely conscious from the assault. He quickly reached into his pouch and pressed Black Widow's emergency beacon. Just in time, too. The super-agent was moving in for the final, finishing blow when a voice yelled out:

ENOUGH!

A shiver ran down Cap's spine. His vision was blurry, but he could still see the unmistakable form of **Arnim Zola!** The villain from Cap's past—who now looked like something from the future—stood before the fallen First Avenger and spoke. "Good evening, Herr Captain. Welcome aboard."

"Zola . . ." Cap hesitated. "You'll never get away with this."

"Ah, ever the optimist," **Zola** said. "But clearly, you are no match for my **TOMORROW ARMY.**

This super-agent who bested you is merely the prototype. Soon, there will be dozens more. Hundreds, even! And no one—not you, or **S.H.I.E.L.D.,** or your mighty Avengers— will be able to defeat them. I will do what **RED SKULL** never could—

I, ARNIM ZOLA, WILL RULE THE WORLD!!!"

"Zola!" One of the scientists quickly interrupted. "Fighter jets are approaching!"

A battered Cap managed a smile.

"This is inconvenient, but not unexpected," Zola replied. He turned to the other scientists. "Evacuate the boat." Zola looked at Cap and gave him *one final blow.*

OOMPH!

17...16...15

14...13...12

11...10..9..

Cap heard the escape subs shoot out from beneath. He then heard a timer ticking down toward zero. As he struggled to remain conscious, he heard a familiar voice.

WHAT ARE YOU DOING? TAKING A NAP?

Falcon was standing before him.

He grabbed Cap and activated his
hard-light wings.

The winged Avenger radioed Black
Widow, who was watching from
the Quinjet high above the boat.
"I've got him," Falcon said.

"Well, what are you waiting for? Get to the main deck and get out of there!" Black Widow yelled.

Falcon grabbed Cap and flew high into the sky.

"Get the medical bay ready," Falcon said as they flew away.

WE'RE COMING HOME!

4..3...2...1

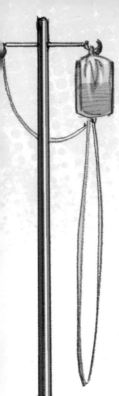

CHAPTER

6

*W*eeks later, Steve Rogers woke up in the medical bay on board the Helicarrier.

"Ugh. . .what hit me?" he asked.

"A prototype **HYDRA** super-agent," Nick Fury said. "Multiple times."

"Thanks for reminding me," Steve said. "I suppose you're here with another mission?"

"No," Fury began. "I'm here to

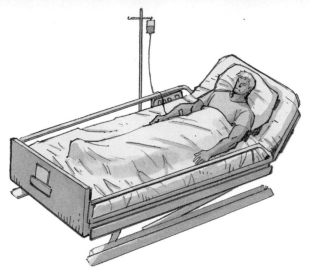

make sure you're all right. You took a bad beating, Captain," he said as he walked over and looked Steve in the eye. "And you used poor judgment. This isn't the same HYDRA you fought during World War II. This is a new-and-improved HYDRA. They adapted with the times. You didn't. Your mission. . .was a failure."

Fury's words hurt almost as much as Steve's wounds. *He's right*, Steve thought. Steve had acted alone instead of accepting help. He'd thought his enemies were just like he was and fighting them would be just like it used to be. But he had been wrong.

"Thanks to the Super-Soldier Serum, you're going to be fine. You should be cleared to leave in another week or two."

"A week? Or two? But what about **HYDRA?"** Steve asked.

"We've learned that **HYDRA** is going to make a move in five days—on the **FOURTH OF JULY.** You can watch the events from your hospital bed," Fury said before leaving.

Steve thought long and hard about what Fury had told him. He wasn't about to let Black Widow, Falcon, and the agents of **S.H.I.E.L.D.** go up against **Zola** and **HYDRA** without him.

But Steve was still uncomfortable in this modern world. He liked the things he knew: the old Times Square, black coffee, his 1942 Harley. If he was going to adjust to the modern world, he would need help, and Steve knew just where to turn. He checked himself out and left to find a friend.

A RED-AND-GOLD BLUR

streaked across the New York skyline and came to a stop atop a glistening state-of-the-art skyscraper. Steve Rogers, with his dented shield slung across his back, walked across the roof and addressed the red-and-gold Super Hero who stood before him.

"Hello, Tony," Steve said to the invincible Iron Man.

"Oh, hey, Cap," Iron Man nonchalantly said as his faceplate lifted to reveal the handsome Tony Stark. "I didn't see you there. WHAT'S UP?"

"IS IT AN AVENGERS MISSION?"

"DOES FURY NEED HELP WITH SOMETHING?"

"ALIEN INVASION?"

"RAMPAGING ROBOTS?"

"MOLE MEN?"

"SOMETHING STUCK IN HIS GOOD EYE?"

"It's not an Avengers mission, and Fury doesn't need help," Steve said. "I do." Tony's smiling face turned momentarily confused, and then Tony invited his fellow Avenger inside **Stark Tower.**

Steve explained everything that had happened in the past few weeks. No details were left out. When he was done, Tony let out a long sigh.

SO WE'RE DEALING WITH AN ARMY OF HIGH-TECH SUPER VILLAINS LED BY A DUDE OLDER THAN YOU WHOSE FACE IS ON A TV IN HIS BELLY?

"You forgot about the Techno-Disruptor, whatever that is. . . ." Steve said.

"Right, it's a device that can knock out and shut down specific technology," Tony replied.

Steve was shocked.

"How do you know all that?"

"I'm a genius billionaire inventor. I know everything," Tony said. "Plus, I hacked **S.H.I.E.L.D.'s** encrypted files last night. Anyway, we've got our work cut out for us. But if anyone can bring you into the twenty-first century, it's me."

Tony continued. "Once we do that, then we'll do something about your horribly

outdated wardrobe," Tony added under his breath. "Then you can hit the town and do the **jitterbug** or whatever the craze was a hundred years ago."

Steve stared at his clothes, unsure whether Tony was joking with him or insulting him.

Tony smiled. **"Come on, Cap, let's go!"**

During the next four days, Tony taught Steve everything he could about the modern world.

EIGHT THOUSAND FIVE HUNDRED SIXTY-SEVEN . . .

And all the while, Steve was getting stronger and healthier. Not only was he doing ten thousand sit-ups and push-ups again by the end of day three; he was also texting. Tony Stark was proud, though there was one major upgrade left.

CAP! CHECK OUT THIS SELFIE!

Tony led Steve into a large room that was part garage, part laboratory, and part man cave—but that wasn't what impressed Steve. The room was lined with new Iron Man armors, all in various stages of development. Tony couldn't help noticing Steve's reaction to all the suits.

202

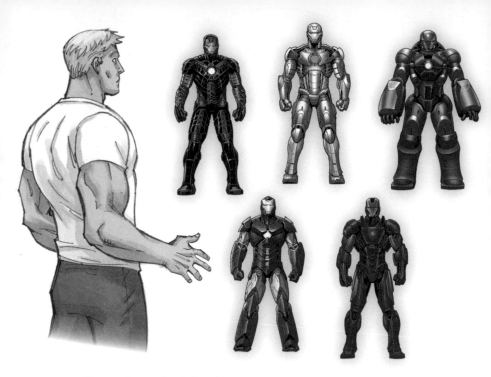

"Cool, right?" Tony remarked. He walked over to Steve's 1942 Harley. "But we're here to discuss this ancient two-wheeled vehicle that may have, at one point, been called a motorcycle."

"Look, I've listened to you on everything else. Don't even try to talk me into a new bike!" Steve exclaimed.

"Do. Or do not. There is no try,"
Tony said, much to Steve's confusion. "What?
It's Yoda. Didn't we get to that? Never mind.
You're getting a new ride, courtesy of me. Or do
you want to have to jump onto another bus?"

Steve looked from his bike to Tony, then
back to his bike. "What did you have in mind?"
he asked.

A wicked smile flashed across Tony's face.
"Two words," he began.

Steve gulped. "All right," he said. "But on one condition: you fix this first."

"My pop made this," Tony said. His father, **Howard Stark,** had crafted Steve's iconic shield. Tony looked at it and understood Steve's connection to the things from his past.

Then that mischievous smile came back to Tony's face. "These little dents? I can bang them out in no time. Then we fix your bike, get you back to the Helicarrier so you can stop **HYDRA,** and still have you home in time to watch the fireworks."

"You want in?" Steve asked. "I could use the armored Avenger when I take on those super-agents."

"Thanks, but I have to be in Europe by midnight. Reports are that Crimson Dynamo has been spotted near Italy—plus, I'd like some gelato for dessert."

And with that, the two heroes got back to work. It was going to be a long night.

CHAPTER 7

*T*he next morning, Captain America found himself again aboard the Helicarrier and inside Nick Fury's office. **"Where have you been, Captain?"** Fury asked, wondering why Steve had checked himself out of the medical bay days earlier.

"I went to see a friend," Steve began. "He helped me get back in the game. I'm ready to take on **HYDRA.** But I'll need a little help."

"You're America's First Super-Soldier and the First Avenger, and it's the Fourth of July," Fury replied as he extended his hand. "You can have all the help you need." The two men shook hands, and it was as if Cap had never left.

"What's the latest intelligence update?" Cap asked.

"Thanks to scraps recovered from the boat and surveillance from our best agents, including Black Widow, we have determined that HYDRA will strike this evening at the very symbol of American freedom: the Statue of Liberty."

"And what, exactly, is Zola's plan?" Cap asked.

IT'S JUST LIKE HE SAID: HE PLANS TO TAKE OVER THE WORLD WITH HIS TOMORROW ARMY.

"Regular men and women have been turned into an unwitting evil army. Those athletes on the bus—the ones you saved on their way to the Yankees game—they were part of **Zola's** plan. They were his test subjects. *HYDRA'S* been kidnapping people and brainwashing them. **Zola's** been downloading *HYDRA* fighting skills and orders directly into their brains and then hooking them up to all this superior, futuristic tech—making them nearly unstoppable."

"And is each one as strong as the prototype I fought?" Cap asked.

Fury nodded.

"And you're sure of their target?" Cap asked.

"Yes. I believe **Zola** wants to make a very public display," Fury responded.

"Agreed," Cap said. He thought for a moment and then added, "I need a battalion of your best **S.H.I.E.L.D.** agents. Black Widow, Falcon, and I will lead them into battle."

Fury flashed a rare smile, suddenly feeling much more confident.

"I'm not done," Cap said, much to the director's surprise. "I'm also going to need some tech."

Nick Fury raised his unpatched eyebrow.

"Did Captain America just ask for tech?" Fury said.

Later, Agent Coulson led Captain America into the Helicarrier's Research and Development area. Cap made his way to the sonic disruptors and precise EMP blasters. "These are all nonlethal and won't hurt **HYDRA'S** unwitting army, but they should do damage against **Zola's** tech," Cap said, much to Coulson's surprise.

"I'll also need a team of our top programmers to be stationed nearby the fighting so they can work on creating firewalls and jamming frequencies to block **HYDRA'S** intelligence network," Cap added. Agent Coulson was clearly impressed.

SO YOU PLAN ON HITTING THEM IN THE VIRTUAL WORLD AND THE PHYSICAL WORLD.

"It's going to be a one-two punch." Cap flashed one of Stark's mischievous grins. "Please have the entire team assembled in the hangar in one hour."

As Coulson saluted his hero, Cap added, "And, Coulson? Thank you."

Inside the hangar, Captain America's team of **S.H.I.E.L.D.** agents and programmers were readying their equipment and suiting up for the battle as Fury watched from the sidelines.

"Welcome back, buddy," Falcon began. "Don't take this the wrong way, but are you sure you're up for this? No one would blame you if you sat this one out. Me and Nat can handle this."

FALCON—SAM—I APPRECIATE YOUR CONCERN. BUT IF YOU'RE GOING AFTER HYDRA, I'M GOING WITH YOU.

"We're just concerned," Natasha said.

"I'm fine, Natasha. In fact, I'm better than fine. Now let's finish this briefing and get down to Liberty Island."

"What about your ride?" Falcon asked. "Do we still have to drag that old bike around?"

"Thanks for reminding me," Cap said. He took a small device out of one of the pouches on his belt and pressed down on its flat screen. There was a beeping sound, then a whirring, then a huge gust of wind. Everyone turned in amazement. The crowd of **S.H.I.E.L.D.** agents was speechless.

Fury looked at Captain America, totally shocked.

BEEP!

TWO WORDS...

SPACE

BIKE!

CHAPTER

8

Captain America, Falcon, Black Widow, and their battalion of **S.H.I.E.L.D.** agents were hidden throughout Liberty Island, waiting for **HYDRA** to make its move.

Just as the sun was setting, they heard a low humming. They looked up to see giant zeppelins floating toward the Statue of Liberty. Then they heard loud splashing sounds and saw vehicles rising from the bay. The invasion had begun.

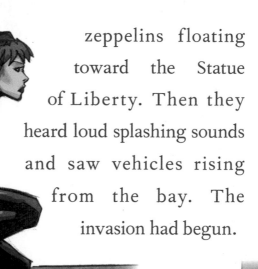

Cap signaled everyone to remain where they were. He wanted the battle contained to the island, so they would have to wait until **HYDRA** disembarked and made the first move. As if on cue, **Zola's** voice reverberated from the lead zeppelin.

ATTENTION! ATTENTION!

> I, ARNIM ZOLA,
> LEADER OF HYDRA, NOW CONTROL
> ALL TRANSMISSIONS.

"I control all information! I control all of you! Today, the world will feel the unmatched power of **HYDRA.** For too long we have stayed hidden in the shadows. Now, we will rise. Now, **HYDRA** and its Tomorrow Army will take its rightful place at the head of the world."

In response, the **HYDRA** soldiers and the brainwashed Tomorrow Army threw their arms into the air and yelled, **"HAIL, HYDRA!"**

Cap gripped his shield and was ready to lead the attack when an eerie green wave of energy shot down from the zeppelin at the statue's crown.

The Statue of Liberty

"They're going to destroy the statue!" Falcon said in a hushed, urgent tone.

"No," Cap replied. "If they wanted to destroy it, they would've done that by now. **Zola** has something else in mind."

"Look!" Black Widow shouted. The beams **Zola** had fired made the statue glow. Then it looked as if the statue was melting. Then, slowly, the statue began to change its shape. "They're using matter reorganizers. Not even Stark has that technology!"

The heroes looked on in horror as parts of the statue transformed before their very eyes. Zola melted the statue's head and spiked crown, then fired the ray again and molded them into a hideous, many-tentacled skull, the very symbol of HYDRA.

"If you cut off one head, two more will grow! HAIL, HYDRA," Zola's voice then boomed from above.

221

Captain America stood horrified by this grotesque symbol of evil. For a split second, he felt utterly defeated. Then, as the last soldiers of the Tomorrow Army emerged from their vehicles and advanced on land, he felt a hand on his shoulder.

"Cap," Black Widow said softly. **"It's time."**

Cap felt hope return.

"Let's go," he said, swinging his shield around and charging toward the statue's base.

ZOLA, YOU AND HYDRA HAVE ONE CHANCE TO STAND DOWN AND SURRENDER. I WON'T ASK AGAIN!

"Herr Captain, so soon recovered, I see," **Zola** said as he leaned out of the zeppelin's window and addressed the Super Hero. **"Wunderbar.** I had hoped you would attend the festivities and the invasion of your precious New York City." **Zola** pressed a button on his wrist gauntlet, and the Tomorrow Army's helmets flashed a brief red light. They had been upgraded with new instructions: commence the attack, and bring Captain America to **Zola.** The fight was on!

In mere minutes, it was clear that **HYDRA** had the upper hand.

Cap radioed the **S.H.I.E.L.D.** tech team stationed on a rooftop in lower Manhattan, led by Coulson. "Coulson, report! Any chance of jamming their communications systems, or knocking them out entirely?"

"We're working on it, sir," Coulson replied. "Their signals are being scrambled, and we've been unable to pinpoint their exact frequency. I need two more minutes."

"The battle might be over in two minutes," Cap yelled. **"You have one!"**

226

HUH?

Cap went back to the battle and threw his shield as hard as he could. It bounced off one, two, three Tomorrow Army helmets, momentarily knocking soldiers down.

Cap reached out to retrieve his shield, but it never returned. Instead, a bigger arm covered in wires and tech had the shield in its grasp. It was the original **HYDRA** super-agent.

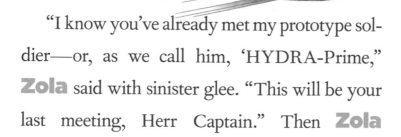

"I know you've already met my prototype soldier—or, as we call him, 'HYDRA-Prime,'" **Zola** said with sinister glee. "This will be your last meeting, Herr Captain." Then **Zola**

addressed HYDRA-Prime. **"Finish them,"** Zola commanded. HYDRA-Prime nodded and advanced toward Captain America.

"Didn't take my advice the first time we met, hmmm?" the villain asked as he threw Cap's shield to the ground.

"Bring it on, pal,"

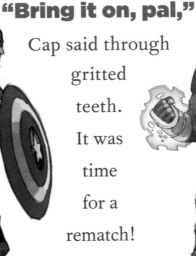

Cap said through gritted teeth. It was time for a rematch!

CHAPTER

9

*H*YDRA-Prime's fist slammed into Captain America's jaw.

CRACK!

WHUMP!

Captain America delivered a powerful kick to HYDRA-Prime's ribs. As the two men continued their knock-down, drag-out fight, **Arnim Zola** grabbed a rope and descended from his zeppelin onto the Statue of Liberty, where **HYDRA** agents were connecting the Techno-Disruptor to the opposite side of the transformed face. **Zola** cackled. "Soon Lady Liberty will be singing out of the other side of her mouth that I am her rightful leader!"

Back on the ground, Cap was out of breath and in pain. He had managed to grab his shield, but he was still losing. **"You are weak, Captain,"** HYDRA-Prime taunted. **"You cannot defeat me alone!"**

"You're so right," Cap said as he clicked on a small homing device from one of his pouches. "That's why I won't repeat the same mistake I made last time. This time I'm not alone!"

Within seconds, Falcon and Black Widow sprang into action. Falcon soared toward HYDRA-Prime as fast as he could, but HYDRA-Prime was faster.

OOMPH!

The two heroes **collided** and **fell** to the ground. HYDRA-Prime merely laughed. **"You will have to do better than that!"**

"Okay, how about this!" Cap said, landing a right hook across HYDRA-Prime's face. Cap quickly turned and regrouped with Falcon and Black Widow.

"You weren't kidding about this guy," Falcon said. "What's our plan?"

Before Cap answered, he hurled his shield at HYDRA-Prime. It smashed into his chest and returned to Cap. HYDRA-Prime staggered back and roared in pain. Captain America had bought them a few seconds of planning. **"I'm his main target,"** Cap said. "I'll provide cover; you two disable his tech—but do it quickly. I can't go another twelve rounds with this guy." Then Cap's eyes suddenly grew wide. *"THAT'S IT!"* he exclaimed. *"BOXING!"*

Black Widow and Falcon looked at him, confused.

"We have to go twelve rounds with him. He won't expect that. He's looking to end this quickly. We've got to fight him like Joe Louis would: methodical and controlled, over and over again."

"That's Joltin' Joe," Falcon quietly said to Black Widow.

"Joltin' Joe was a baseball player, genius, not a boxer," Black Widow corrected. **"Now look alive— here he comes!"**

The Super Villain charged toward them, then pointed his hands in their direction and fired bolts of electricity from his fingertips.

Cap raised his shield and deflected the bolts right back at the villain, temporarily distracting him. Falcon and Black Widow used the distraction to their advantage. Falcon fired his grappling hook and wrapped it around the villain's high-tech boots, tripping him up and sending him crashing to the ground.

As he fell, Black Widow fired her stingers

directly at the side of his helmet in hopes of damaging the wires that connected it to the chest piece.

HYDRA-Prime staggered again and was knocked back by a spinning red, white, and blue blur. As Black Widow and Falcon attacked from the side, Cap charged from the front. As they fought, each hero took a turn leading. When HYDRA-Prime turned to face one of them, the other two heroes would jump in. Falcon and Black Widow followed Cap's lead, and soon the three heroes were working in unison. Their attack was methodical and controlled, and they were wearing down HYDRA-Prime.

HYDRA-Prime lunged at Cap. The villain swung and missed, and Cap knew it was time for the final strike. Captain America jumped on top of the villain and grabbed the now damaged wires tightly with both hands. Then, using every ounce of strength in his Super-Soldier body, he ripped them out.

HYDRA-Prime let out a loud scream before collapsing to the ground, defeated.

"You did it!" Falcon yelled to Cap.

"We did it!" Cap quickly corrected.

"But it's not over yet. **Zola's** still standing. We have to stop him—and fast!"

"I can reach the top of the Statue of Liberty in twenty seconds," Falcon said as he began to extend his hard-light wings.

"Too slow!" Cap replied as he pressed a remote. His space bike streaked through the sky and then down toward the heroes. The First Avenger jumped in the air, grabbed the handlebars, and steered the bike straight up toward **Zola.**

As Cap approached the crown,

YOU ARE TOO LATE,

Zola quickly grabbed a gauntlet from one of his fallen Tomorrow Army soldiers and fired bolts of electricity toward Cap. Cap dove the flying motorcycle out of the way, then revved its engines and sped through an opening in the crown. He jumped off the hovering bike to face **Zola.**

"Once again, you are too late, Herr Captain. I have already won," **Zola** said as the Techno-Disruptor next to them sprang to life!

Just then, Cap heard a transmission from Coulson:

CAP—WE'VE FIGURED OUT HYDRA'S TECH! WE CAN SHUT IT DOWN AND DISABLE THE TOMORROW ARMY!

But energy waves had already begun to cascade from the device toward Manhattan. Slowly, all technology began to fail and shut down, including **S.H.I.E.L.D.'s** tech! Cap's flying motorcycle crashed to the ground with a loud **THUD**. He had to destroy the Techno-Disruptor—**now!**

Captain America advanced toward **Zola,** determined to stop him and the device. The villain cackled. "Fool! Your Super-Soldier strength is no match for my genius intellect! I control it all, Herr Captain! And he who controls technology controls the future!"

"And those who don't learn from the past are doomed to repeat it!" Cap replied. He grabbed **Zola** and lifted him high above his head, throwing the Hydra leader through the air.

244

Zola landed with a *SMASH* and fell back, sliding out of the crown.

"Admirable, Herr Captain, but you have only slowed me down," the villain said.

Cap ignored him and flung his shield. It whizzed across the crown and landed with a **ZING** in the side of the Techno-Disruptor. The machine sputtered and sparked, but it wasn't enough to stop it. Cap pulled his shield from the machine and ran toward his space bike. "Guess we're going to have to do this the old-fashioned way."

Cap tried to
activate the flying
motorcycle but it
was no use. Thanks
to the Techno-Disruptor,
it had no power. But Cap just grinned
and flipped a switch. Pieces of his bike
flew through the air. Beneath the high-tech
exterior was a fully functioning old-school
motorcycle!

Cap grabbed a cable from the side of the

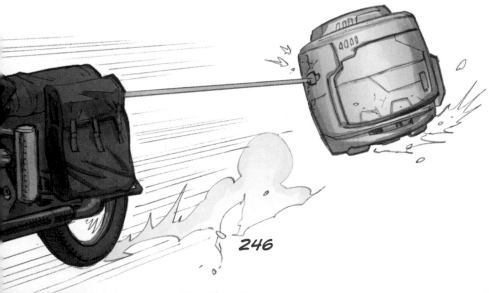

bike and attached it to the machine. Then he jumped on the starter and revved the engine. Cap took a deep breath and gunned his bike, riding it—with the machine attached—straight off one of the tentacles.

Cap—on the motor-cycle with the machine still attached—flew high into the air, then started falling to the island below.

It was Falcon! As he soared toward Cap, the First Avenger jumped off the bike. Falcon caught him just in time, and they flew high into the air, the bike and the Techno-Disruptor exploding below!

The explosion was spectacular! Disabled by the **S.H.I.E.L.D.** team in lower Manhattan, the entire Tomorrow Army collapsed to the ground. When Coulson got the all clear from his men, he fired a single flare into the night: mission accomplished!

Somewhere along the East River, a New Yorker saw the explosion, then the flare, and decided to shoot his own fireworks into the sky. He was quickly joined by another New Yorker across town. And another. And another. And another.

Soon the sky was filled with explosions signifying the triumph of good over evil.

"'And the rockets' red glare, the bombs bursting in air,'" Cap said quietly to himself.

"We did it," Falcon said. "We stopped **HYDRA.**"

"And protected life, liberty, and the pursuit of happiness," Black Widow added.

"Yes, but **Zola** got away," Cap said as he began to walk through the wreckage. "He's not here. And neither is HYDRA-Prime."

SLITHERED AWAY LIKE THE SNAKES THEY ARE.

STILL, THE GOOD GUYS DID WIN.

NICE WORK, TEAM. HAPPY FOURTH OF JULY!

CHAPTER

10

*T*he next morning, Steve Rogers woke up before his alarm. He got out of bed, stretched, and began his morning routine. He did his usual push-ups and sit-ups and soon began his morning run through Manhattan.

Steve's body ached from the battle the night before, but he was happy. He had saved the day. As he ran, he looked around Times Square. One of the giant screens was broadcasting familiar footage.

The news anchor announced, "Captain America saves New York!"

He ran downtown and stopped by Old Joe's for his morning paper, smiling at the headline.

"NICE JOB," Old Joe said. "I gotta tell ya, I was scared until I saw you on the scene."

"I was scared, too, Joe," Steve replied.

Steve headed to the trendy coffee shop and went inside. Everyone was talking to each

other about what had happened the night before. Some were huddled around cell phones looking at pictures of the battle, and others were sitting at tables deep in conversation, but they were all connected—all bound by the same unbelievable events that had happened on the Fourth of July.

Steve stepped to the counter and saw the kid from the last time he had been there. Much to Steve's surprise, the kid remembered him. **"HEY, CUP OF JOE, BLACK, RIGHT?"** Steve nodded. "Coming right up, Cap!"

As Steve waited for his coffee, a few people came up and asked to take pictures. Others patted him on the back or shook his hand. After a few minutes, Steve paid for his coffee and sat on his usual bench outside. He looked across

the water at Liberty Island.
Construction crews were
already hard at work fixing
the statue. Scaffolding rose
as high as the crown.

Then Steve looked around. He saw kids pretending to be Super Heroes. A young couple were walking down the street holding hands, and he overheard them say how happy they were that Cap had saved the day. They didn't know that Captain America was sitting just a few feet from them. The city was bustling with energy, and all was right with the world.

Steve was happy to be alive. Thanks to the past few weeks, Steve had learned to appreciate what he had but also remember what had come before. He realized that he had to adapt with the times instead of living in the past. He also realized the importance of friends, and of working together and asking for help. Steve let out a contented sigh of relief. Then he heard a beeping sound.

Steve lifted the cell phone Tony Stark had given him and saw a text from Avengers Mansion. It read:

Steve tapped the screen and was soon staring at Sam Wilson's face on his phone. "What's the situation?" Steve asked.

"It's Batroc," Sam began. "You, me, and Natasha are back in action. And I think we're going to need the others."

Steve smiled. "Text me your coordinates, and tell the rest of the Avengers to stand by to assemble," he said.

"I'M ON MY WAY!"

INVASION OF THE SPACE PHANTOMS

STARRING

IRON MAN

BY STEVE BEHLING

ILLUSTRATED BY

KHOI PHAM AND CHRIS SOTOMAYOR

MARVEL

Los Angeles
New York

FEATURING YOUR FAVORITES!

IRON MAN

ALIAS

TONY STARK

CAPTAIN AMERICA

FALCON

HULK

M.O.D.O.K.

NICK FURY

BLACK WIDOW

A.I.M. AGENTS

ROBOT SHARKS

PHANTOMS

OUTPOST 13

S.H.I.E.L.D. AGENTS

ALIEN DOGS

LIVING SNOWMEN
(NOT REALLY)

COSMIC BRIDGE
GENERATOR

THE STORY OF IRON MAN

*I*nventor. Pioneer. Genius. **Tony Stark** is all of the above, and he'd be the first to say so! In fact, he's much more. But let's not get ahead of ourselves.

After the unfortunate death of his father, Howard Stark, Tony became responsible for his father's megasuccessful company,

STARK INDUSTRIES, at only twenty-one years old! Stark Industries developed and built state-of-the-art weapons and sold them around the world. Tony didn't care what happened to the weapons after they were sold; he just wanted to be rich!

Then one fateful day, during a top-secret weapons test, Stark was ambushed by a gang of heavily armed criminals and taken prisoner. He was critically wounded and told he had only a short time to live. With Stark weakened, the criminals forced him to build a weapon for them—a weapon of mass destruction. But Stark had other plans! He forged an incredible suit of armor and a miniature arc reactor to power it and keep his heart beating.

With his new arsenal, Stark defeated the criminals and escaped. He vowed from that day forward that he would use his scientific knowledge to help people all over the world. He upgraded the suit of armor and became the invincible **IRON MAN**!

Iron Man joined Black Widow, Captain America, Hawkeye, the Hulk, and Thor to form the **AVENGERS**— a team of Earth's Mightiest Heroes dedicated to saving the world.

CHAPTER 1

"Is MY BOW TIE STRAIGHT? TELL ME MY BOW TIE IS STRAIGHT," Tony said with a groan. *Standing around shaking hands and saying, "Great to see you!" to people I don't even know is hardly my idea of a good time*, he thought. *I'd rather armor up and throw down with the* **Crimson Dynamo***!*

Happy Hogan, Tony's bodyguard, let out a loud sigh. "You aren't wearing a bow tie, Boss. Remember? You said you didn't want to look like me." Happy fidgeted in his tuxedo, nervously fixing his own crooked bow tie.

"Right, right. So remind me why I agreed to come to this thing?" said Tony. Just then, a voice thundered through the ballroom's public address system.

"Welcome, everyone, and thank you for attending the inaugural benefit for the **Holistic Plan for Tomorrow**!" The crowd of well-dressed partygoers burst into applause as a large hologram of an older man appeared in the center of the room.

"While I am sorry that I am unable to attend in person, I wanted to thank you all for coming. As you know, the Holistic Plan for Tomorrow—**H.P.T.**—is dedicated to opening new doors for the future. With your generous donations, we will create a world the likes of which no one has ever seen!"

The hologram's voice and face belonged to the mysterious **Elton Traggeore**, a reclusive billionaire who was the president of H.P.T.

"HEY, HE'S A RICH GUY, JUST LIKE YOU," said Happy, laughing. "Do you know him?"

"It's not like there's some rich-guy club, Happy," said Tony, rolling his eyes. Happy raised an eyebrow. "Besides, no one's ever met Elton Traggeore."

Before Happy could reply, he and Tony heard a familiar voice. **"Mr. Stark?"**

Turning around, Tony found himself face to face with **Agent Phil Coulson**, a member of the top-secret organization known as **S.H.I.E.L.D.** Coulson smiled at Tony and Happy, gesturing toward the ballroom's exit doors.

"I know that smile," said Tony with a sigh. "That's your 'I'm smiling but I'm not really smiling' smile."

"Would you mind coming with me?" asked Coulson. He pointed once again to the exit.

Tony nodded for Happy to stay as he and Coulson walked out of the ballroom and into the long, crowded entrance hall. Tony spoke quietly. "So what does **S.H.I.E.L.D.** want with Mr. Doesn't-Play-Well-with-Others?" asked Tony. "You guys lose the **Hulk**?"

Coulson looked at Tony. There was no longer a smile on his face, forced or otherwise.

OUTPOST 13

"No," replied Coulson. **"Black Widow and Falcon."**

"Wait, what? *Really?*" said Tony loudly. People in the hallway turned his way suddenly.

Coulson looked down at the ground and whispered, **"We have a . . . problem at OUTPOST 13."**

To the public, it was known as **U.S. SCIENCE FOUNDATION OUTPOST 13**. The scientists there, tucked away in the wastelands of Antarctica, claimed to be studying astronomy and surveying the vast shelves of ice. In reality, **OUTPOST 13** was home to an ultra-secret **S.H.I.E.L.D.** research lab.

And that research lab was currently testing a *marvelous* new device . . . invented by Tony Stark.

"Define 'problem,'" said Tony, his curiosity piqued.

"We hadn't received a transmission from Outpost 13 in over a week—but then one came. They kept repeating the words MONSTER and HELP. **Director Fury** sent **Black Widow** and **Falcon** to investigate, but we haven't heard from either of them in forty-eight hours."

Tony stared at Coulson. Falcon and Black Widow were his friends. They were also forces to be reckoned with. Now they were missing. . . .

"I'll go," said Tony. "I can get there faster than anyone."

"Not just you. **You** *and* **Captain America**. You'll rendezvous with Steve Rogers at approximately—"

THuD!

Before Coulson could finish, Tony headed toward the parking lot, where a **STARK INDUSTRIES** vehicle waited. As Coulson picked up his pace in pursuit, Tony opened the trunk of the shiny red car.

"I hear you, Coulson," said Tony, without looking back.

"You have really loud shoes."

THuD! THuD! THuD! THuD! THuD!

"Mr. Stark, it's vital that you combine your efforts with **Captain America**," said Coulson as he approached. "This is more than one Avenger can handle . . . even *you*. We sent both Black Widow and Falcon—two of **S.H.I.E.L.D.**'s best—and now they're **MIA**. You'll *need* Rogers on this." Coulson shifted his feet uncomfortably. "Maybe even the **Hulk**."

Without warning, various pieces of metal flew from the trunk toward Tony, attaching themselves to his hands and feet. Within seconds, Tony was encased in a nearly impervious **suit of armor**.

"The research being conducted at **OUTPOST 13** . . . if it should fall into the wrong hands . . ." said Coulson. He glared at Stark, as if he knew exactly what the genius inventor would say.

"I know  all about the research, Coulson. They're using my technology. And if Widow, Falcon, or anyone else is hurt because of me, it's my job to make things right."

Where there once stood a billionaire inventor now stood the invincible

IRON MAN!

As the armor powered up, Tony's mind raced. Years before, he had become Iron Man when he realized **STARK INDUSTRIES'** technology could be used to hurt others. He had since dedicated his life to helping humanity. And now he was faced with a situation where all his efforts could be undone.

"Mr. Stark, wait!" yelled Coulson, but his plea was ignored.

"The *right* hands will make sure the *wrong* hands don't get away with anything. Tell your boss not to worry. It's nothing Iron Man can't handle!" With that, he activated his boot jets and blasted into the night sky.

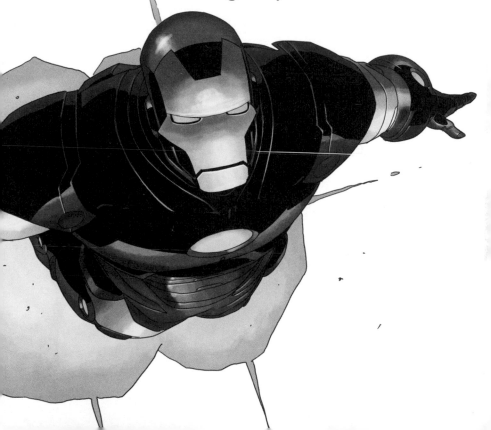

CHAPTER 2

*I*t took Tony a little under six hours' flight time to reach snowy Antarctica. He surveyed the desolate surroundings via his helmet's heads-up display and asked **J.A.R.V.I.S.** to give him the lowdown on the area.

"Temperature: zero degrees Fahrenheit. Atmospheric conditions: currently snowing. Expected snowfall: six inches. Barometer holding st—"

"J.A.R.V.I.S.," said Tony. "Scratch the weatherman bit. How about we start with signs of life?"

A brief humming followed, and *J.A.R.V.I.S.* spoke once more. "Approximately three point two miles southwest.

"_MULTIPLE HEARTBEATS DETECTED—"

Black Widow, Falcon, the scientists . . . and what else?

"—**LIFE-FORMS UNKNOWN.** I'm receiving significant signal interference," finished J.A.R.V.I.S.

"Don't tell me," Tony continued.

"IT'S THE NIGHT OF THE LIVING SNOWMEN, RIGHT?"

"Impossible. It is currently four p.m. local time. And snowmen are not living entities," *J.A.R.V.I.S.* answered.

Ignoring his armor's operating system, Tony activated his boot jets and unleashed a chemical thrust that propelled him into the air.

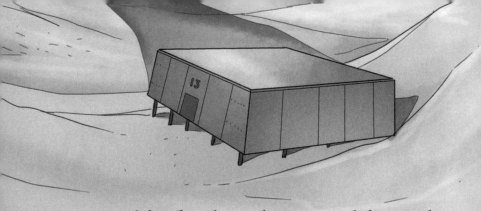

He used his hand repulsors to stabilize and took off in the direction *J.A.R.V.I.S.* had indicated. The heavy snowfall made flying by sight nearly impossible, but his armor's navigation systems quickly took over. Tony zeroed in on a small clearing, where the burnt remains of a rectangular building, with portholes placed every few feet, stood on scorched stilts.

OUTPOST 13.

Tony's armored boots crunched through the snow as he approached the main entrance to the outpost. A chill crept up Tony's spine, and it wasn't from the cold.

No smoke, thought Tony. *This fire happened at least a day ago.* Immediately, his thoughts went to Black Widow and Falcon. *Without the proper gear, surviving the harsh Antarctic environment even an hour is a challenge, let alone two days.* . . .

As Tony approached **OUTPOST 13**, his audio sensors picked up a sound . . . distant and muffled tapping, gaining speed and getting louder, something—some*things*—slamming into the metal interior walls with tremendous force. Suddenly, the door flung off its hinges and three large sled dogs burst from the entrance to **OUTPOST 13**. The canines barked aggressively and bared their fangs. **Their eyes glowed a sinister deep red.**

"Whoa, nice doggies!" said Tony, holding his palms out toward the canines. "Uh, roll over! Fetch?" *Where's a stick when you need one?* he thought, moving forward. Before he could take another step, one of the dogs jumped and slammed into his armor, knocking him down. Tony scrambled to his feet as another dog smashed his helmet with its giant front paws. Then the remaining dog started VIBRATING and SHAKING, and one of its large forepaws MORPHED into a long TENTACLE! The appendage wrapped around Tony's right arm and squeezed the armor so tightly that it started to bow and bend under the pressure.

"I don't have dogs, but they don't usually have tentacles, right, *J.A.R.V.I.S.*?" asked Tony.

"AFFIRMATIVE, SIR."

At the *SPEED OF LIGHT*, Tony sent a volley of repulsor blasts from his wrist gauntlets in all directions, causing two of the dogs to scatter behind the outpost, howling. Meanwhile, the third dog continued to squeeze Tony's right arm with its snakelike appendage.

"You can ... let go ... anytime you want!" said Tony as he held his left gauntlet right above the dog's limb and emitted a controlled repulsor burst from his palm. The dog let out a shrill squeal and uncoiled its tentacle from Tony's arm.

I'm beginning to see why Coulson was so worried, Tony thought. *If this is just the welcoming committee ...*

The canines continued to change shape, growing in mass until they were nearly three times their original size, with eight tentacles each. They were greenish yellow in color, with glowing red eyes, and their mouths had **barbed tonguelike projections**.

As Tony struggled with his foes, he caught a fleeting look at a face gazing out from one of the outpost portholes. Then another. He looked again and they were gone.

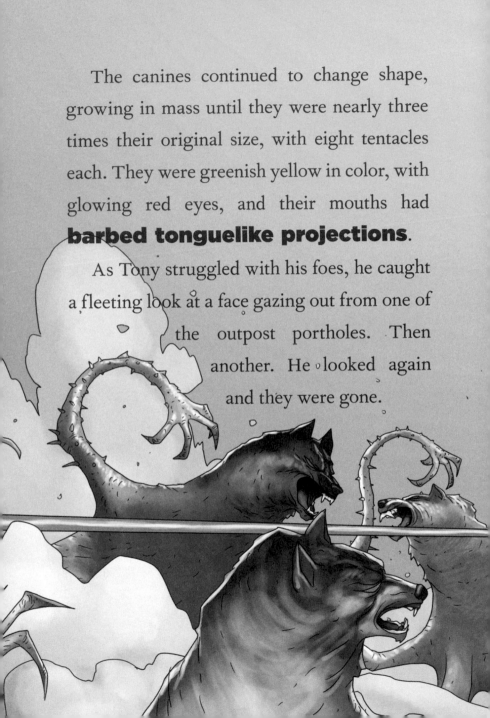

Tony was only minutes into the mission, and the situation was deteriorating rapidly. Dogs that evolved into weird octopus creatures? He worried that these were the threats **Black Widow** and **Falcon** had faced. And could those faces he'd seen belong to some of the missing scientists?

The questions were piling up!

Thinking fast, Tony fired rapid repulsor bursts at the ice mounds the creatures were using as protection, causing them to dive out of the way. Next he fired a blast at a metallic cylinder that extended from **OUTPOST 13** into the ice below, ripping open an Iron Man–size hole. Then he activated his boot jets, thrust himself past the beasts, and soared into the cylinder.

said Tony as a brilliant blast of heat issued from his armor's unibeam, sealing the cylinder from the inside.

"This was either a really good idea or a terribly bad one," he said with a laugh. He proceeded through the cylinder and into the darkness below . . . **alone**.

CHAPTER 3

*I*ron Man landed at the bottom of the metallic cylinder and found an opening that led to a hallway of corrugated metal. Dim yellow lights dotted either side of the hallway.

"*J.A.R.V.I.S.*, those things back there. Any idea what they were?" said Tony as he entered the below-freezing hallway.

"*SCANNING DATABASE. RESULT: NEGATIVE. IT MUST BE SOMETHING WE HAVEN'T ENCOUNTERED YET,*" replied *J.A.R.V.I.S.*

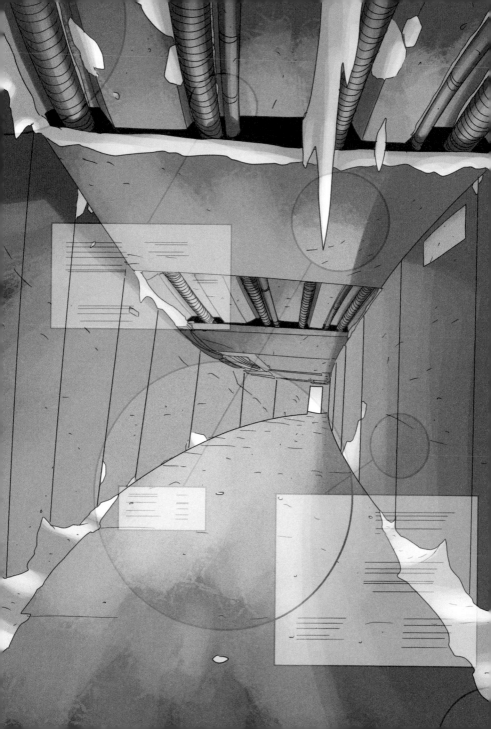

"It must be," said Tony, sighing heavily as he continued down the hallway. He reached a door with a sign above it that read **VAN WALL RESEARCH CENTER**. Curious, he entered, using his helmet's visual scanners to assess the large room. Heavy machinery lined the walls, and a bank of computers that rivaled anything on the **S.H.I.E.L.D.** Helicarrier stood in the middle. The scanners revealed energy **WAVELENGTHS** that were familiar to him.

As Tony walked toward the computers, **J.A.R.V.I.S.** blared in his ears: **"LIFE-FORM DETECTED."**

Whirling around, Tony zeroed in on a metal storage unit in a far corner. He was getting a little tired of this game of **hide-and-seek**.

"Whoever's in that cabinet can come on out," called Tony. "It'll save us both some time."

The cabinet door whipped open, and out staggered a frumpy middle-aged man.

"IRON MAN!" he said, running toward the armored Avenger.

Iron Man steadied the man, bracing his shoulders with both hands. Tony decided to slide his metal visor back, revealing his face. "Take it easy, **Dr. . . . Blair**," said Tony as he read the badge on the man's lab coat. "Where are the missing scientists? Where—"

Blair grabbed Iron Man's wrist, tugging him in the opposite direction. **"I'm the only one! We need to leave, now!"**

"You're safe, Dr. Blair," said Tony, trying his best to sound reassuring. "I need some answers. **Where is everyone? What were you working on?**"

The doctor wrung his hands nervously, sweating profusely. "Our—our research . . ." he stammered. **"The Cosmic Bridge Generator—"**

"A portal," interrupted Tony, **"to another, unseen dimension.** A way of harnessing extraterrestrial power sources for the benefit of everyone on Earth."

Blair nodded. "The first test knocked out our communications. We spent days trying to get them up and running. That's when Black Widow and Falcon arrived. **Without warning, they attacked us!**"

J.A.R.V.I.S. suddenly spoke in Tony's ear. "I am detecting a rise in Dr. Blair's blood pressure and heart rate."

He's lying, thought Tony. *Why would Black Widow and Falcon respond to the distress call only to turn around and attack a bunch of scientists?* ***Something's not right. . . .***

Suddenly, a blast of energy hit Tony squarely in the chest plate, knocking him off balance. A glance at the doorway revealed the source of the attack—**Black Widow**. It must have been Tony's imagination, but she seemed so angry her eyes glowed red! Swooping in above her came **Falcon**.

"Black Widow! Falcon!"

Tony faced his teammates. "Coulson's been looking everywhere for you two. What is going on here?

"Ease up, it's me!"

Without a word, Widow fired more bursts from the Widow's Bite gauntlets she wore on her wrists. Intense electric bolts attacked Tony's armor. Various internal alarms sounded, and Tony glanced at his helmet's heads-up display. "'Power cell A compromised'?

That can't be good," said Tony as he crouched in a defensive posture.

"I just had this suit polished!" Tony shouted at Black Widow. His faceplate slid into place, forming the visage of Iron Man. Black Widow said nothing, keeping her glare and her gauntlets trained on him. Falcon's shadow circled them.

"I thought we were fighting on the same team, or am I wrong about that?" Iron Man said, trying to reason with them. But he was met with only an eerie silence and red eyes. Those piercing red eyes. *It's like they're not themselves! Black Widow and Falcon would never*

WHERE'S CAP WHEN YOU NEED HIM?

*attack a friend like this. What happened? Or . . .
what happened to them?*

"Get behind me, Doc!" shouted Iron Man.

The room seemed to spin as **Black Widow** and **Falcon** circled Iron Man and Dr. Blair. Tony took a big gulp. *"It's nothing Iron Man can't handle."* Me and my big mouth.

307

CHAPTER 4

*I*n the confines of the **VAN WALL RESEARCH CENTER**, Tony was at a disadvantage. Between Black Widow's blasts and Falcon's swooping, circling, and smashing, Tony was getting crushed. Just as he'd right himself, he'd be hit with another attack.

The ceiling was high but not high enough for powered flight. Falcon could glide, so he had the tactical advantage. Black Widow used her expert acrobatics and leapt across the enormous machines that lined the walls.

Tony just couldn't match the speed
and agility of Black Widow or Falcon.
On top of that, the only way he could
defend himself was to hurt his friends. But
what kind of friends attacked their own?

"Multiple life-forms detected," declared
J.A.R.V.I.S., distracting Tony for a moment . . .
which was all Falcon needed to swoop down
and grab Iron Man. Falcon flung Tony into
a solid granite wall.

Then came the sound of something hurtling through the air, followed by metal hitting metal.

Tony looked up to see a familiar **RED, WHITE, AND BLUE** uniform standing before him. **Captain America!** Black Widow and Falcon turned their combined gaze on Cap.

Cap adjusted the shield on his left arm, deflecting one of Widow's blasts. "I was supposed to catch a ride with you," Cap said.

"I was just on my way to pick you up," Tony said with a sigh of relief.

"I'm glad to see you found Black Widow and Falcon. **They just don't look too glad to see you. . . .** Did you find the scientists?"

"Negative," Tony answered. "Not sure if you noticed, but I've been a little busy fighting our 'friends.'"

"Point taken . . ." replied Cap.

Falcon and Black Widow charged toward them. Cap used his mighty shield to block the two and send them flying.

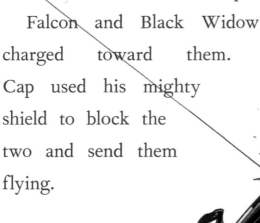

"Those two seem very interested in this,"
said Cap, motioning to a circular framework at
the center of the room. Inside the framework
was a large gateway—big enough to fit the
Hulk—surrounded by a series of metal beams
that protruded at odd angles. Within the gateway was a swirl of light
against dark, color
against black. It
looked like the
universe itself
was con-
tained there.

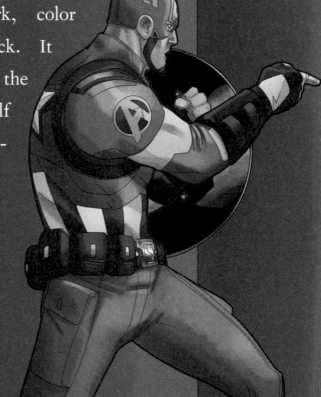

Eyes . . . eyes . . . thought Tony.
Eyes! That's it!

"Cap! You notice something off about Widow and Falcon?" he asked.

The sentinel of liberty stood his ground, deflecting Widow's attack while taking note of everything around him. It was a skill honed in combat, from his days battling **RED SKULL** and **HYDRA** to his time fighting alongside the mighty Avengers. "Their eyes," Cap answered with authority. "They're red!"

"Good guess!" said Tony. "I owe you shawarma when we're back in New York. Now I've got a hunch. . . ."

Without skipping a beat, Captain America extended his right arm with incredible force, throwing his shield directly at

HELP! HELP! HELP!

THUMP! THUMP!

Falcon's hard-light wings. "Play your hunch!" he called. "I'll draw their fire!"

That's when Tony heard it—a distant thumping, mixed in with what sounded like moans or cries for help. *The scientists? Maybe I* did *see their faces before. They must be nearby!*

While Captain America fought, Iron Man moved to the metal gateway in the middle of the room. Tony flipped up the cuff on his right gauntlet to access a touch pad. Moving his index finger along the pad, he hacked into the generator's controls. Tony was now in command of the machine.

It glowed purple, then green, and finally red, crackling with orbs of black energy.

"Hey! Bad teammates! Over here!" shouted Iron Man, waving at Black Widow and Falcon.

The generator pulsed, red light illuminating everything in the room. Bathed in the light, Black Widow and Falcon cringed, their shapes shifting then returning to normal. The red light glowed stronger and stronger, and its effect on Black Widow and Falcon grew stronger, too!

Without warning, Iron Man zapped Black Widow and Falcon with his repulsors, knocking them in front of the Cosmic Bridge Generator. In a flash, they both vanished from view.

"Did we just lose Black Widow and Falcon . . . again?" Cap said, shaking his head. "Fury won't like this. What's going on, Tony?"

Iron Man looked at Cap, then at the generator. He had gambled with the lives of people he had known for years. If he was right, then everything would be fine. But what if . . .

What if I was wrong? he thought. *What if I made a mistake?* **What if I have *lost* Black Widow and Falcon . . . *forever?***

CHAPTER

5

*T*he Cosmic Bridge Generator quivered and hummed, its crimson glow permeating everything around it. Captain America ducked behind his shield, eyes closed tightly. Even then he could see the brilliant red light coming from the generator. Tony lowered polarized lenses over the eye ports on his helmet. He couldn't escape the otherworldly red, either.

"There!" said Iron Man as he tapped a sequence into the keypad on his right gauntlet.

He sounded more confident than he felt. Just as quickly as it had started, the generator powered down. **The quivering and humming stopped, and the red glow faded.** Raising the polarized lenses inside his helmet, Tony looked toward the generator. Standing before it were two figures. *What if I just made everything worse?*

"Anyone get the license plate of that truck?"

asked Falcon, rubbing his head. Beside him stood Black Widow. Both heroes looked stunned, unsure of their surroundings.

"You guys all right?" asked Iron Man as he turned to face Widow. He was relieved to see that her eyes were back to normal. Tony Stark raised his visor and grinned. *That was close. . . .*

"I'm fine, Tony," answered Widow. "I just can't remember anything that happened since we arrived at **OUTPOST 13** and were attacked."

Falcon nodded. "Last thing I remember is entering **OUTPOST 13**. We were ambushed by a beast with lots of long slimy arms. Then there was a flash of red, and the next minute—**WHAM**—here we are!"

"Someone activated the generator and it knocked you guys out and sucked you inside . . . into another dimension," Tony explained. "The Falcon and Black Widow who attacked me and Cap? **Doppelgängers. Duplicates. Imitations.**"

The heroes swiveled their heads in unison as they heard the generator hum back to life. Standing in the breached wall was Dr. Blair, looking panicked. He was moving his finger over a device that resembled a wristwatch.

"Can you shut that down, Doc?" groaned Tony.

"WE'VE HAD ENOUGH FUN WITH THIS DOOHICKEY TODAY."

"You have to stop them, Iron Man!" blurted Dr. Blair, sounding hysterical. "Those two destroyed Outpost 13! They captured all the S.H.I.E.L.D. scientists!"

"Who's this quack?" asked Falcon, jerking a thumb at the doctor.

Black Widow studied Dr. Blair carefully. "I've never seen you before," she said warily.

Dr. Blair looked at Tony, shaking his head. **"Don't trust them, Iron Man! They were so quick to turn on us before, so ready to attack! What if they do it again?"** He slowly started walking toward Tony.

"Take a deep breath, Doc," said Tony.

The doctor eyed Black Widow and Falcon with suspicion. **"You have to destroy them, Iron Man—**while we still can!"

"Doc, you really need to relax! The Black Widow and Falcon we were fighting before were imitations. These are the real deal."

"Yes, they are," grunted Dr. Blair.

Blair's arm suddenly turned into a tentacle and grabbed Iron Man, smacking him to the ground! The appendage dripped with thick slime and left a sticky green residue on

everything it touched. Wrapping around Iron
Man's helmet, the tentacle began to squeeze
tighter and tighter.

As Tony struggled to free himself, the
Avengers raced to his side. More tentacles
exploded from Blair's body and snaked out in
all directions, stopping the heroes dead in their
tracks. Unleashing two repulsor blasts that hit
Blair in the stomach, Iron Man knocked the
doctor back into the massive machinery. Blair
eased his grip just enough for Tony to escape.

Dr. Blair's shape began to SWELL and DEFORM like a marshmallow in a microwave oven. The mass reformed until it was a large yellow-green blob with eight long appendages. Its eyes glowed red with hate.

"That's something you don't see every day," said Falcon.

The creature unleashed TWO ARMS at **Black Widow**, trying to wrap them around her wrists. But her lightning-fast reflexes kicked in, and she fired off several shots from her Widow's Bite gauntlets. The electric bolts hit the creature and scorched its tentacles.

The beast LASHED out once more, this time at **Captain America**. In one

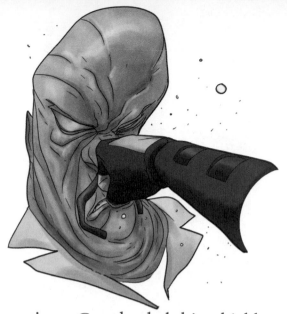

fluid motion, Cap hurled his shield at the creature's head and then hit the ground in a somersault, ducking below its eight limbs. Cap came out of the roll and firmly planted his fist in its face.

The pulsating mass towered over the Avengers and spoke with venom. "I AM NOT OF THIS WORLD."

Tony walked closer to the creature as the other Avengers closed in behind him, ready for battle. **The Cosmic Bridge Generator** hummed. "This," began Tony, nodding toward the apparatus, "is pretty important to you, huh?"

The twisted shape spat out its barbed tongue in disgust. "YOU'LL HAVE NO ANSWER FROM ME, HUMAN."

Its raspy voice made Tony's flesh crawl.

"Fair enough," Tony concluded, then whirled around and blasted the generator to pieces with his repulsors. Captain America hurled his shield, smashing the flying debris. As Tony's visor slid into place, Iron Man and

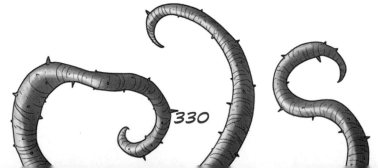

330

the creature continued their face-off.

The creature smiled. "Do you think that is it?" it hissed. "We are great in number, human! Even as I speak, we near the completion of a new Cosmic Bridge Generator, large enough to bring all of my kind to this pitiful speck of a planet. WE WILL DESTROY ANYTHING IN OUR WAY!"

CHAPTER 6

The room fell silent. The **AVENGERS** stared at the monster before them. No one said anything, but Tony knew what they were thinking: if he hadn't invented the **Cosmic Bridge Generator**, Tony and his teammates wouldn't be staring down the barrel of the end of the world.

I created the generator to do good, Tony thought. *Now it's being turned into something terrible. All right, Mr. Guy-Who-Can-Fix-Anything. How do you fix* this?

Before he could continue his thoughts, Tony heard a banging sound once more and what could have been a muffled cry for help. *The* **S.H.I.E.L.D.** *scientists!* Tony finally pieced together what had happened at **OUTPOST 13**. *These creatures must have captured the scientists and kept them around in case anything went wrong with the generator. They're here somewhere!*

Tony turned to Black Widow and Falcon and with a nod motioned them to the slimy yellow-green beast's side. "Mind telling us what that sound is, gruesome? I'm betting it's the missing **S.H.I.E.L.D.** scientists. Be a good little monster and show us where they are."

"It matters little," sneered the creature as it folded two of its tentacles together. "YOU CANNOT STOP US."

"Yeah," said Falcon. "We've heard that one before."

Black Widow and Falcon grabbed the hideous monster and pushed it into the hallway outside, demanding that it lead them toward the captured scientists.

Iron Man stared at the smoldering ruins of the generator. "The more I think about it, there was no way the scientists and that creature could pull this off alone," he mused. "They had to have had help. Someone good at sci crime, maybe."

"'Sci crime'?" said Cap, puzzled.

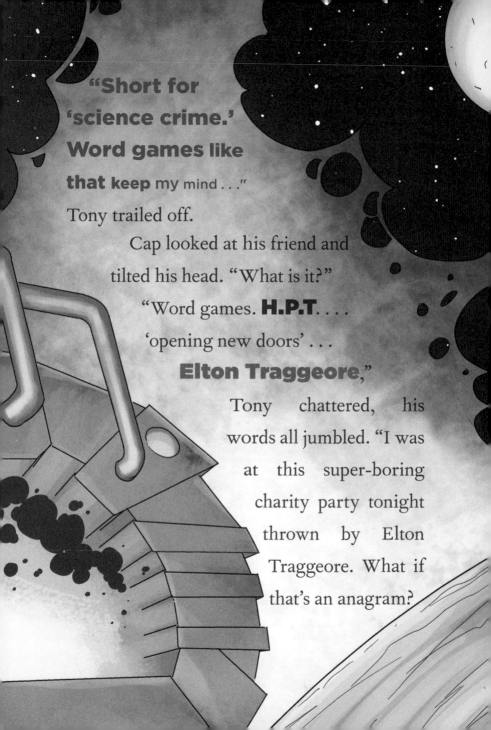

"**Short for
'science crime.'
Word games** like
that keep my mind . . ."
Tony trailed off.

Cap looked at his friend and
tilted his head. "What is it?"

"Word games. **H.P.T**. . . .
'opening new doors' . . .
Elton Traggeore,"

Tony chattered, his
words all jumbled. "I was
at this super-boring
charity party tonight
thrown by Elton
Traggeore. What if
that's an anagram?

"Rearrange the letters in Elton Traggeore and you get another name: **George Tarleton**. George Tarleton, as in . . ."

Cap and Iron Man looked at each other and spoke in unison:

"M.O.D.O.K."

By the time **Iron Man** and **Captain America** caught up with Black Widow and Falcon, the two heroes had found and freed the missing **S.H.I.E.L.D.** scientists. Two of the scientists, Agent MacReady and Agent Childs, were prepping a cryo-containment unit to hold the creature. The unit—a sleek translucent tube with metal caps—would keep its occupant in a state of suspended animation:

alive, **asleep,**

and unable to do any damage.

The monster fixed its eyes on Agents Childs and MacReady. Tony approached from behind and opened his chest unibeam, which unleashed a blast that knocked the monster into the cryo-containment unit. The creature bounced back immediately, and Tony gulped. *No one gets up from a full unibeam hit that fast. Not even Thor.* "PATHETIC EARTHLING. NOTHING YOU DO CAN STOP US. NOTHING!"

"Childs, MacReady, get this thing out of here!" said Tony.

"With pleasure," Childs replied as she activated the cryo-containment unit. With a *whoosh*, the unit sealed itself, flash-freezing the monster inside. Anti-gravity discs beneath the unit turned on and the capsule **HOVERED** just above the floor.

"One alien on ice ready for transport," said MacReady. He and Childs gave the unit a push and slowly maneuvered it out the door.

Tony's mind turned to **M.O.D.O.K.** The villain never worked alone.

A.I.M. and **M.O.D.O.K.** Two of Iron Man's oldest enemies.

A.I.M.

ADVANCED IDEA MECHANICS

was a criminal organization that used science for evil. It was that science that had transformed a lowly A.I.M. agent named George Tarleton into **M.O.D.O.K.** He had then turned the tables on A.I.M., using his superintelligent brain to take over the organization. M.O.D.O.K.'s mind powers could be deadly, and everyone knew it. The A.I.M. agents obeyed his every order. Luckily, sensitive scanners in Iron Man's armor could locate M.O.D.O.K.'s energy signature and track him anywhere.

Tony paused and looked down at his armor-covered hands—the brilliant crimson gloves that could forge reality from dreams. But dreams could become nightmares. An unfamiliar feeling seized him: guilt.

I invented the generator. And now the bad guys are going to use it to mess with the earth. This is all my fault. I have to fix this mess myself.

"All right, people," Cap ordered. **"We need a battle plan and—"**

"Plan whatever you want," said Tony, cutting off Captain America. "I'm taking **M.O.D.O.K.** down. Now."

BATTLE PLAN:

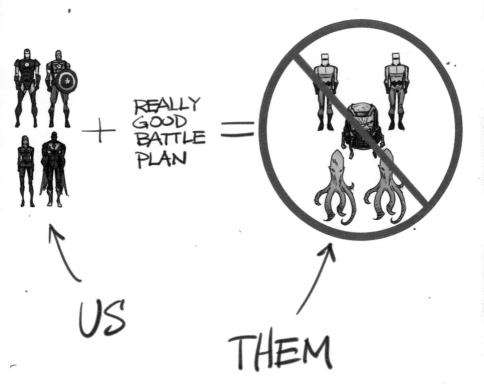

US

REALLY GOOD BATTLE PLAN

THEM

THIS IS *TOO* BIG FOR ANY ONE OF US, TONY!

The high-pitched whine of Iron Man's boot jets kicked in, and Cap jumped back. He yelled over the sound of chemical thrust, "You can't defeat M.O.D.O.K. by yourself!"

But Tony wasn't listening. The armored Avenger blasted off, arms outstretched, and used his repulsors to smash through the roof above.

Iron Man was gone!

CHAPTER 7

"*E*TA, J.A.R.V.I.S.?" asked Tony, sweating inside his armor despite the temperature control.

"ESTIMATED TIME OF ARRIVAL THREE MINUTES, THREE SECONDS," J.A.R.V.I.S. replied.

Tony checked his visual scanners as he skimmed the surface of the Atlantic Ocean— low enough to evade any **A.I.M.** radar. Almost as if on cue, A.I.M. Island appeared on the horizon.

"Let's go for a swim, *J.A.R.V.I.S.*," said Tony. In response, J.A.R.V.I.S. immediately prepped the armor for underwater maneuvers. All openings were sealed; carbon dioxide exhaust ports were activated.

Tony plunged into the ocean.

Why did I snap at Cap back there? he thought.

Tiny caterpillar drives—silent engines—turned in Tony's boots, propelling him toward A.I.M. Island with stunning speed. In the quiet ocean void, Tony gave himself over to his thoughts. ▬—○—▬

I wasn't angry with him. I was angry with myself. None of this is his fault. If I hadn't built the generator in the first place, those aliens wouldn't be trying to take over the earth. And M.O.D.O.K. *and* A.I.M. *wouldn't be helping them.*

Once again, Tony was overwhelmed with guilt. How could he continue to invent advanced technologies but also guarantee they would be used only for good and not evil— **to help others, not hurt them**?

He checked his oxygen supply— 85 percent. So far, so good. The armor's motion detectors revealed three objects circling in the distance. Sharks, maybe? But *J.A.R.V.I.S.* hadn't detected any life-forms. ROBOT SHARKS, *I bet. Of course* A.I.M. *would have robot sharks.*

*Why didn't I listen to Cap instead
of running off on my own?*

Tony activated his armor's underwater countermeasures, and several small robotic beacons ejected from his shoulder launcher. Each mimicked the sounds of Tony's armor and drew two of the robot sharks away. The third shark was HUNGRY . . . for metal! It attacked Tony from below and almost swallowed him whole! THE METAL TEETH GROUND AGAINST HIS ARMOR, and his suit began to fizzle and cave in on him. Tony quickly grabbed the robotic jaws and activated his elbow thrusters, tearing the metal mouth in two.

Really? Tony thought. *I almost bit the bullet because of a* ROBO—FISH? He rocketed like a torpedo toward his destination.

Beneath the ocean, ▓▓▓▓ Island looked like a large geodesic dome constructed of foreign materials—nothing like the islands Tony was used to vacationing at.

This is where Cap would say, **"We need a plan. We need to act as a team,"** thought Tony. *And here I am with neither. Well done, Stark, well done.*

"Okay," Tony said to himself, "time to make a door."

"They kind of give me the creeps," said the A.I.M. agent with a shudder. She stood with another agent at the door of a large control room.

"Shhhh," the second agent replied softly. "Don't let the boss hear you talking like that!"

ZAAAAAAK! The wall ripped open, torn apart by a massive repulsor blast! In rushed a torrent of seawater and, along with it, Iron Man! The agents were knocked unconscious. An alarm wailed for only a second before it was silenced by Iron Man's repulsor.

Let's hope I didn't wake anybody up, he thought.

Within minutes, the wall had resealed, leaving no sign of Iron Man's entrance. **"Self-healing polymer walls,"** said Tony. "We'll have to look into those for Stark Tower. Save a fortune every time the Hulk busts a wall."

Iron Man was inside **A.I.M.**'s hidden base, in a **twisting** corridor. Activating his boot jets, Tony took off, continuing to follow **M.O.D.O.K.**'s energy signature.

The master control room is enormous, Tony thought. He was up in an air shaft, looking down at the room through a grate. He saw an assembly of **A.I.M.** agents—all armed—surrounding an enormous duplicate **Cosmic Bridge Generator**.

"You are too cautious," said a spine-chilling voice.

"And you are not cautious enough!" came the reply, silencing everyone in the room.

Tony took a second to place the first voice, but he knew the second one. . . . **M.O.D.O.K.**

Iron Man smirked. He was confident he had the element of surprise. He prepared to blast through the grate, but before he could act, an explosion struck Tony's hiding spot. He fell to the floor of the master control room, hard.

"You're late, Iron Man," **M.O.D.O.K.** intoned. He almost sounded bored. **"I EXPECTED YOU APPROXIMATELY THIRTY-FOUR SECONDS AGO."**

Iron Man righted himself and was greeted by the army of **A.I.M.** agents. Floating beside them in his hover chair was M.O.D.O.K. His head was impossibly huge and his limbs tiny, almost useless. In the center of his vast forehead was a glowing beam, the source of his immense psionic powers.

"I would have been here sooner, but the traffic was terrible," Tony joked. He tried to sound like his usual devil-may-care self, but the odds were against him. Things didn't look good for one lone Iron Man.

M.O.D.O.K. ignored Iron Man and hovered over to the generator's control panels. Iron Man saw the familiar yellow-green blobs, their many arms reaching, grabbing, constructing. This new Cosmic Bridge Generator dwarfed the one Tony had destroyed at **OUTPOST 13**.

"That thing looks big enough to, I don't know, bring a whole planet of slimy, scummy creatures to Earth," said Tony. Channeling as much power as he could to his repulsors, he unleashed a barrage of devastating blasts at the generator. Well, they should have been devastating. Unlike the generator at **OUTPOST 13**, this one was unaffected by his repulsors.

One of the beasts let out a bitter laugh, then slowly shuffled its mass toward Iron Man. Its writhing arms shot out and grabbed

Tony by the neck. Then, without w a r n i n g , it dropped him and began to change shape. Its features slowly morphed, going from altogether alien to a little more . . . familiar.

Two arms, two legs. Tall. Elongated facial features. Almost human.

Something Tony had seen years before.

356

"Phantoms?" said Tony in disbelief. Back when the _AVENGERS_ had first joined together to fight evil, he had encountered a strange being who called himself the Space Phantom. He could change his shape to mimic almost anyone or anything. He imitated the different members of the Avengers, pitting the heroes against one another.

"Yes, that is what your kind call us," snarled the alien, its voice practically dripping with slime. "Our own world has become . . . inhospitable. But your world . . . your Earth . . . will make a glorious new home. Once you and your miserable kind have been . . . displaced."

"Slow down, sloppy joe. What about all the nice people who already live here?" Tony asked. The A.I.M. agents began to circle Iron Man. Tony's audio sensors detected the sound of their weapons heating up.

"The Phantoms shall first replace all those humans in positions of power," M.O.D.O.K. explained. "Your Cosmic Bridge Generator will transport the Phantoms here and send their human counter-parts to their destroyed home world."

That explains why they needed

the generator! Every time a Phantom imitates someone, that person is sent to the Phantom's world. But when a Phantom changes its shape again, the person returns. They would need some other method to send people away permanently . . . *like the generator!*

"And what's in it for you and A.I.M.?" Tony asked M.O.D.O.K.

M.O.D.O.K. threw Tony a look of annoyance. **"IS IT NOT OBVIOUS? I DESIRE COMPLETE CONTROL OF THIS WORLD.** With the Phantoms, that goal is within my grasp."

Tony had heard enough. He ordered J.A.R.V.I.S. to switch all energy reserves to his repulsors. But just as he was about to unleash all the force he could muster, he was struck by the **A.I.M.** agents! They fired at once, encasing him in a field of hard light.

Then **J.A.R.V.I.S.** came online with more bad news: "Power now operating at reserve levels."

M.O.D.O.K. and the Phantoms closed in on Tony.

He struggled against the onslaught, but he could still hear Cap's words echoing in his head:

This is too big for any one of us, Tony.

CHAPTER 8

*T*he heads-up display inside Tony Stark's helmet was full of alarms, warnings, and worse. Systems were malfunctioning. Circuits were overloading. Tony knew his armor was crashing.

"You delay the inevitable," muttered M.O.D.O.K., who hadn't even bothered to join the fight. The A.I.M. agents' new weapons were doing a good job of destroying Iron Man's armor all on their own. And the Space Phantom smirked at Tony all the while, confident that soon his comrades would begin their takeover of Earth.

"J.A.R.V.I.S.! Reroute all remaining power to the unibeam!" shouted Tony.

"REMAINING POWER REROUTED," said J.A.R.V.I.S.

"Good. Stand by to detonate

unibeam on my mark!"

Then it happened—so fast that neither **M.O.D.O.K.**, the Phantoms, nor the **A.I.M.** agents could process it:

Tony ejected himself from the Iron Man armor and threw himself across the room, clear of the hard-light bubble and away from his foes.

The armor remained inside the bubble and the unibeam exploded with pent-up energy, shattering its hard-light prison and bathing the room in a shockwave that floored everyone and everything.

—o—

A dazed Tony Stark was the only one who had seen the explosion coming, and even he was surprised. *Who knew it would work that well?* thought Tony. He had deduced that the hard-light bubble was keyed to his armor and his

armor only—so ejecting himself from the armor effectively freed him. And by rerouting all the power to his unibeam, Tony overloaded the armor, causing it to self-destruct. He had bought himself precious time but at a price.

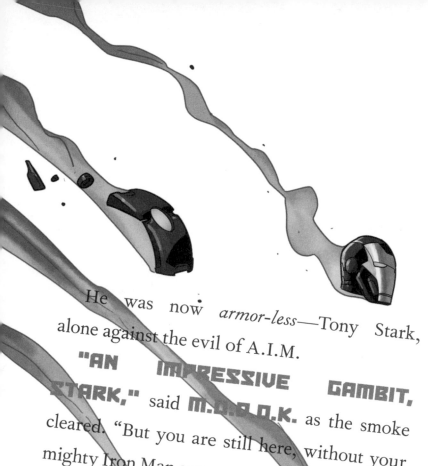

He was now *armor-less*—Tony Stark, alone against the evil of A.I.M.

"AN IMPRESSIVE GAMBIT, STARK," said M.O.D.O.K. as the smoke cleared. "But you are still here, without your mighty Iron Man armor. Surely a man as smart as you knows when to admit defeat."

Tony crouched behind a rack in the corner of the room. *I may not have my armor, but I'm still Tony Stark*, he thought. *And the day I let a bunch of beekeepers, goofy aliens, and a giant head stop me will be the day I can't memorize pi to seventy thousand places.*

"SHOW YOURSELF, STARK!" called **M.O.D.O.K.** "It is hopeless! Surrender now and I promise you a slow, agonizing death."

"That all sounds great, M.O.D.O.K.!" Tony yelled. **"It's a tempting offer, but I'll pass!"**

Tony was in trouble and he knew it. If only he had listened to Cap.

And that's when he heard it—**a distant rumbling**. The rumbling got **louder** and

louder. Everything in the room began to shake. Tiles fell from the ceiling and pillars toppled. Behind M.O.D.O.K., the wall burst in a great explosion!

Standing in the ruin was a large brutish figure, dripping wet, fists clenched. Through gritted teeth, the green-skinned monster snarled, "Puny wall."

OW

CHAPTER 9

"*H*ulk!" yelled Tony. The giant looked at Tony and grimaced. Or maybe it was a smile. It was kind of hard to tell. **"Smash!"**

The **Hulk** ran head-on into the sea of **A.I.M.** agents, their weapons blazing. The Hulk shrugged and tossed agents left and right. One landed next to Tony.

"Enough!" commanded **M.O.D.O.K.**, and his voice seemed to fill every part of the room. A beam of light issued from his headband, blasting the Hulk in the face. The Hulk roared in anger, then collapsed to the ground, holding his head.

A Phantom turned toward the **Cosmic Bridge Generator**. It moved its fingers over the watch on its wrist and the generator came to life. It glowed red, and creepy humanoid shapes began to emerge from within.

More Phantoms.

"Good to see you guys!" said Tony as the Phantoms advanced toward him.

"Who are you talking to, human?" asked a Phantom as it morphed its arm into a tentacle and wrapped it around Tony.

Tony gasped, **"Over . . . there."**

The Phantom sneered, "What are y—" then caught Captain America's shield in the face and lost its grip on Tony.

"We didn't follow you all the way from Antarctica to let one of those things get you," said Cap as **Falcon** and **Black Widow** took the fight to **A.I.M.** Tony smiled at his teammates. *I'm one lucky shellhead*, he thought, *lucky to have friends who've always got my back*.

"Never mind that," replied Tony. "*These* aliens plan on using *this* generator to invade our world!"

"So let's blow it to pieces!" said Black Widow, knocking an A.I.M. agent to the ground.

"Tried it. It's made out of some kind of material that isn't **blow-up-able**."

"Is that even a word?" asked Falcon, punching an **A.I.M.** agent through the helmet.

Cap smiled at Tony.

"So if force alone won't do it, what will?"

"Teamwork," offered Tony.

"We can start by helping the Hulk. Can you take out M.O.D.O.K.'s psi-beam?"

After assessing the situation, **Captain America** had only to look at **Falcon**.

With the speed of his namesake, Falcon swooped in from above, raking one of his hard-light wings against **M.O.D.O.K.**'s face. His attack against the Hulk cut short, M.O.D.O.K. found himself face to face with Falcon's fury!

The **A.I.M.** agents scrambled to aid their
fallen leader, but they had their own problem
in the form of **Black Widow**! Like a
one-woman wrecking crew, she tore through
the agents. Using all the martial arts prowess at
her command, Widow attacked relentlessly,
never slowing.

"Cap! I know how we can stop these guys . . . but I'm gonna need your help," said Tony. The two raced toward their green-skinned teammate.

"That's what friends are for," said Cap.

———○———

Cap and Tony were cut off from the Hulk. A line of Phantoms formed between them, shape-shifting into gruesome monsters. They looked like dinosaurs gone horribly wrong. Sharp talons, fangs, spiked tails, and long sinewy limbs. The creatures let loose an unearthly sound and continued to close in on the heroes.

"Puny monsters," growled the Hulk, smashing his enormous fists into the ground and sending the creatures flying.

"Can you keep these things busy, Hulk?" asked Tony. The Hulk grunted, grabbing one of the Phantoms by its tail. He whirled it around his head, then let go.

"So that's a yes," said Tony. **"Come with me, Cap!"**

Captain America ran alongside Tony and they slid to a stop at the base of the generator.

Tony shook his head. "The generator can transport *things* from the Phantoms' home world to Earth and vice versa. **But what happens if we program the generator to transport *itself*?**"

"I give up," Cap said. "What happens?"

"I don't know," replied Tony. **"But I'll bet you a brand-new space bike the Phantoms will hate it."**

—◉—

A no-holds-barred brawl raged in **A.I.M.** headquarters. **M.O.D.O.K.** tried in vain to hit Falcon with his psi-beam as the winged hero circled above. Black Widow continued her assault against the A.I.M. agents. There were only a few left standing at that point. Meanwhile, the Hulk smashed monster after monster.

I'll need you to throw your shield into the generator on my mark!" shouted Tony. Cap just looked at him. "Don't worry, you'll get it back!"

The star-spangled Avenger moved like a **RED-WHITE-AND-BLUE** blur, knocking back the alien invaders. "Whatever you're going to do, do it fast!"

Tony's fingers raced along the generator's controls. *Just a few seconds,* thought Tony. *Just a few seconds . . .*

"NOW!" cried Tony, and Cap hurled his shield into the Cosmic Bridge Generator just as the giant machine hummed to life. The shield hit the crackling red energy, and the entire room glowed red.

—◯—

As the red veil lifted from the room, Tony Stark looked around. He saw Cap's shield resting on the floor. The generator was gone— and along with it, every last trace of the

Phantoms . . . and M.O.D.O.K., too. All that remained were the Avengers and the defeated agents of A.I.M.

"Well, what do you know," Tony said. "It worked!"

"What did you do?" asked Cap, picking up his shield.

"I used your Vibranium shield to reflect the generator's energies on itself," Tony explained. "The generator has transported itself, along with the Phantoms and M.O.D.O.K. . . . somewhere in space and time."

CHAPTER

10

A few hours later, Tony Stark and Steve Rogers found themselves in an elevator aboard the **S.H.I.E.L.D.** Helicarrier. As the doors to the Helicarrier bridge opened, Tony and Steve walked inside. As usual, the place was buzzing with activity. Standing in the middle of it all was **Nick Fury**, the director of **S.H.I.E.L.D.**

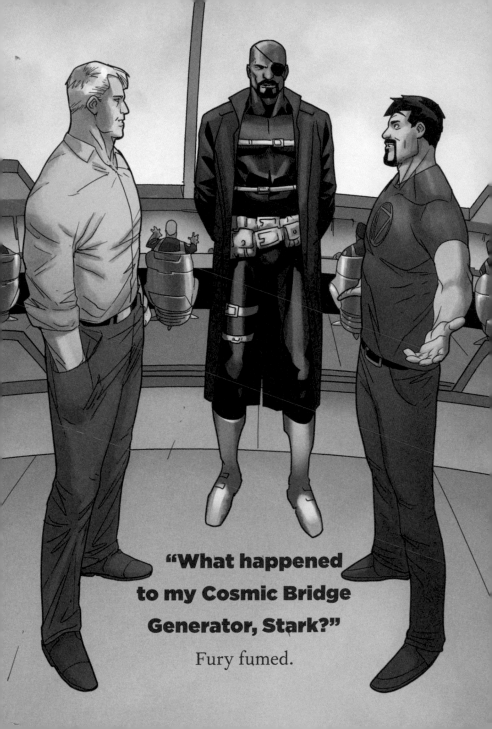

"What happened to my Cosmic Bridge Generator, Stark?" Fury fumed.

"Hi, Nick. How was your day?" Tony replied. Fury just stared at him.

"Technically, it's *my* generator. I made it," said Tony. "Since nobody could play with it nicely, I did the responsible thing. I took my ball and went home—so to speak."

"You're just lucky you stopped another alien invasion," Fury responded, turning his attention back to the bridge. "Otherwise, I might be mad. Plus, you

saved all of those brainwashed scientists."

"At first those scientists were creepy, but they were actually an impressive bunch. Oh, and I hate to correct you again, but *I* didn't stop another alien invasion and save Earth. *We* did. You know, teamwork?" Tony said.

"Go make yourself useful, Stark," said Fury with his back to Tony. And though Tony couldn't see it, Nick Fury smiled.

━●━

Tony took in the view from the **S.H.I.E.L.D.** Helicarrier's observation deck. He could see all of New York City. Among the skyscrapers, he saw *STARK TOWER*. Home.

Amazing, thought Tony. *All of this would have been ruled by a bunch of pointy-headed aliens because I had to do everything on my own. Without the Avengers, my invention could have wiped out our planet.*

"Is this a party of one, or can I join you?" Steve Rogers stood in the entranceway to the observation deck.

Tony nodded at his friend and motioned for him to come in. **"Definitely. I think that 'party of one' thing is played out."**

"We got lucky today," said Steve. "We saved everyone at **OUTPOST 13**, and **S.H.I.E.L.D.** has taken the A.I.M. agents into custody. All that *and* we sent **M.O.D.O.K.** and an army of evil aliens packing."

"**M.O.D.O.K.** will be back. He always comes back," said Tony softly. He looked out at the city and folded his arms. "We would have been luckier if I had listened to you and Coulson."

Steve grinned warmly. "It never hurts to have a plan, and friends to make it happen."

"Y'know, Rogers, if this Super Hero thing doesn't work out, you could make a lot of money writing greeting cards," Tony said with a laugh.

It sounded lame, but Steve was right. Some problems couldn't be solved by Iron Man alone, no matter how many repulsor blasts he fired. Maybe flying solo wasn't always the solution. Tony was part of a team—the mighty Avengers. He had their backs, and they had his.

There just might be something to this teamwork thing, he thought.

Motioning with his thumb toward the door, Steve said, **"Come on. You owe me shawarma *and* a new space bike."**